Bittersweet

Moranda Jane

Published by Veracity Publishing Company

Published in the United States of America by Veracity Publishing Company

PO Box 481703

Concord, N.C.

veracitypublishingcompany@gmail.com

ISBN:

DEDICATION

To my Godmother Katie who read my first manuscript many yeas ago and did my first edit. Though there was a lot of red on the page you pushed me to keep going and encourage myself. Thank you for always being a fount of wisdom and encouragement. Rest in power!

To my older sister Yolanda who brought home books during her freshman year at A & T and encouraged me to read. Thank you for igniting a spark and introducing me to Zora Neal Hurston. But most of all, thank you for challenging me to see different perspectives!

Last but not least, to my baby sister Karen ala Cletus. Thank you for always being a feist taking out ankles when necessary when I needed it most. Thank you for always being one of my biggest cheerleaders. I love you little sister!

TABLE OF CONTENTS

ACKNOWLEDGMENTS

Through HIM that I live, move and have my being I give all the honor and glory for without him I would be nothing.

To the man that I am blessed to wake up to every morning and the guardian of my heart. My Protector who stands as my armorbearer against the world for the woman he cherishes. I thank God daily that you are in my life. Even though you are mean to me (LOL) you continue to push me to be better. I could never repay you for helping me achieve my dream.

To my "besties" Latonia and Ramona who originally kicked the tires on my stories and gave honest feedback on the characters- Thank you!

To my travel partners Shelia and Deon who helped a broken-hearted girl get back in the saddle and helped seed some the adventures that I write about.

To my mommy Evelyn and my first love- my papa Willie Kid Thank you for always encouraging me to have a voice. You raised me to know that there was never any doubt about how much you cared for and loved your middle child!

I'm sure I missed some folks so charge it to the mind and not the heart.

May the Lord bless and protect you; may the Lord's face radiate with joy because of you; may he be gracious to you, show you his favor, and give you his peace.

Numbers: 6:24-26

PROLOGUE

Zalmon Invictus LeBlanc aka Vic

Zalmon Invictus LeBlanc the third of his line, speed along I85, in the back seat of his black Range Rover, mind racing as fast as the traffic whizzing by his window. He needed to be at the Ritz-Carlton in downtown Charlotte to meet his grandmother in twenty minutes and Zalmon was on fire. In his opinion the whole trip was a waste of time. He had more important issues to deal with! They had one job… and they blew it. All they had to do was grab the old lady and the kid and take them to the safe house like he'd requested. He was surrounded by incompetence!

The old woman, but specifically that little girl, was the key to keeping his little guppy on the hook. In the three years in which he'd worked with Cassius Hewson, Vic had averaged seven million a year. Money that was his very own and not a part of his family business. There was no way anything was going to get between him and his money. Right now, he had bigger issues and he needed to be on his A game.

The Old Battle Axe was in town and she never traveled. Something was up and nobody was talking. Maybe she was going to pressure him again into getting married. That shit was for the birds. He was nowhere near the marrying age in his opinion!

North Carolina had been his stomping ground for years. He attended North Carolina Central for his undergraduate and Wake Forest for his graduate and law degree. Born in Florida but raised in the Caribbean, Vic enjoyed all the perks of his dual citizenship. Vic had made a lot of connections during his time in school.

Since his father had stepped up to take the reins, the family had seen an increase in profits. However, the relationships that Vic had forged while attending school helped secure some of the deals that were made. If not for he and his father, the family would be in shambles.

According to his assistant, he was to meet his grandmother for a quick coffee and then they would transition to the place that had been arranged for the meeting. It was odd really because normally they would have just set something up at their main Charlotte office in one of the conference rooms or Rhoda's office. At this point, none of it mattered. He just wanted to appease his grandmother so that they could get on to the business at hand. It wasn't that he didn't love his grandmother Rhoda, it was just she was old, and it really was time for her to sit down. For now, he had to wear the mask. At least until the time was right.

CHAPTER 1

Assembling the Pieces

Zebulon Zelinka

On his reconnaissance trips to keep tabs on the woman that he loved, Zebulon had discovered Edith's. The building wasn't anything fancy, but it didn't need to be. The food served spoke for itself. Anytime he was in Kannapolis, it was imperative that he stopped in for a bite and today was no exception, especially since it would be a long time if at all that he came back this way. So that's where he and his grandson Fernando Zebulon White, or Z as he affectionately called him, met to go over last-minute details of the plan.

Everything was falling into place as expected. The White Rose was returning from Vegas in the next few hours and had made her feelings clear about what steps were to be taken. Those poor sons of bitches won't even see the blade coming.

Grabbing his cup of coffee, Zeb smiled and searched for Matthias. Inhaling its rich aroma, Zeb relaxed back into his seat looking at his grandson. Judging by his afterglow his mission must have been successful. He smiled, lips hovering over the cup. He wanted nothing but the best for his legacy. Though he wasn't happy at first with his choice of mate. Zeb knew in his heart that Adelinda or Del as his grandson called her would protect his grandson with her last breath – hell he would do the same. The sad thing was that his grandson was, and had been at times, way more vicious than he could ever be.

Fernando was a replica of the man that raised him and his namesake in both visage and character. Papa Z was not a man to be trifled with and neither was Fernando. Zeb grimaced at the thought because some of the savagery that Z had acquired could be laid at his doorstep. Fate had left his daughter and his grandson unprotected and if not for the kindness of Andino's. Zebulon shuddered to think of what could have happened. That's what he liked about Del. She not only protected him but also softened his edges. The ironic thing was that Del, through her best friend Charleston, was now living on the Andino estate.

Matthias came around the corner with a pad in his hand, and a pencil behind his ear. Never forgetting a kind spirit, Matthias smiled and offered, "What can I get you, gentlemen?"

"We'll both have Edith's Special. Cheese on the eggs – scrambled soft. Cheese, onions, and mushrooms in the hash browns. No toast, but can you put pecans in the waffles?"

"Y'all not hungry, are you?"

"Well now that you mention it, does your mother still make those wonderful scones?"

"You know it!"

"We'll need three blueberry and three cranberry orange, along with some of her homemade icing."

Zeb turned to his grandson, "You haven't lived until you've had an

Edith scone."

Matthias chuckled, "Today is your lucky day. Mom hasn't baked in a while but today she felt the urge."

"How's she doing?" Zebulon asked with serious concern. Smiling, Matthias responded, "She had slowed down for a while, but over the last few weeks she said she felt a surge of energy."

Zebulon was happy to hear it. From time to time he would pop into Kannapolis to check on the woman that he loved but could never have. She never knew he was even in town, but he had to see her and the boys to make sure that they were safe. During those brief visits, there were many an early morning he found himself sitting with her and some of her fresh baked goods and a cup of coffee. They had some of the best conversations!

Z looked at his grandfather, slight quirk hovering around his mouth, and without asking automatically knew what the deal was. Yeah, they'd eat well now, but he'd have his ass in the gym before nightfall. While Z was taller than his grandfather, Zebulon Zelinka was built like a tank and age hadn't slowed that down.

Matthias walked back towards the kitchen to put the order in and both men used the absence of conversation to check in on the business; phones out using them like mini laptops. Looking up at his grandpa, Z smiled receiving his cousin Kedar's text.

"Looks like our mission is almost complete."

Zebulon nodded his head, calculating what were days but now hours he had left in North Carolina. The life he led did not allow dust to settle under his feet. It had been a long time since he had felt peace like this. He finally fulfilled the one thing he had been yearning for, to tell the woman his lungs breathed for what lie in his heart.

Zeb knew his chances of taking Earlene Andino away from her family were about as successful as an ice cube on Satan's toenail.

Hell, he chuckled to himself with the pun intended, he would never try. It was clear that his love would always be unrequited, but his soul couldn't rest until he told Earlene just how he felt. He did and he would always cherish those moments, feeling her in his arms, his hands clutching her waist, swaying to the beat of LTD and the smooth tones of Jeffery Osborne. Those stolen moments in time would have to sustain him because they were all he'd ever have.

Turning his mind and sight back to his grandson, he asked the question that had been plaguing his thoughts since he'd stepped into the restaurant, "Have you told your beloved about her brother yet?"

Kedar Zra

Kedar checked his watch and noted the time. There was an hour left on the flight, and Kedar still had a lot of work to do. He had kept his puppet jumping long enough, and it was time to end this little game they were playing. His sources in North Carolina informed him that Nora had landed and was frantic. It was a cruel lesson to learn, but he really wasn't a bad guy. His cousin, on the other hand, was not so nice.

Kedar had gotten a call from his uncle Zebulon about two years ago basically informing him to watch the company he kept. The only new stallion in Kedar's fold was Cassius Hewson. Zebulon Zelinka never gave a second warning. So Kedar began to dig. By the time he was finished he knew about the human trafficking, the exclusive After Hour Pop-Ups, and which houses held the safes in which Cass had been hoarding the cash he was making from the businesses.

What he found turned his stomach. The only bright side to meeting Cass was Asa Altman. It was by accident really. He was at an art exhibit in Charlotte and was fascinated by some of the pottery presentations and wanted to see if he could meet the artist and commission her to make some pieces for his home. He had no idea that he would meet the woman who would immediately become the object of his affection. She was enchanting and captured his heart at hello. Within twenty-four hours he had a file which connected her to Cassius. Cassius had kept his jewel hidden only taking Nora out in public. Like her artwork Asa was a rare find. In Kedar's eyes, she was an innocent and should have never been mixed up with a dumbass like Cassius.

Asa was the catalyst for all of this. On some level, Kedar recognized what he was doing this for a woman who didn't even know that he existed until a few days ago was something that her husband or lover should be doing, but from Kedar's perspective, she was worth it. She reminded him of the two people he admired most in this world: his mother Lalanie and his Grandmother Rhoda. Asa was hardworking, caring, and beautiful, but most of all compassionate. He wanted her. It was that simple and that complicated.

In his world she would wilt, so he just admired her from a distance. It was why he installed the security cameras at her house. She needed to be protected. For all the good it did. The fox still got in the hen house. Cassius may have thought he was sly as a fox, but his cousin Zalmon Invictus LeBlanc III aka Vic was a snake.

Kedar was a Leblanc by blood. His father was Edom LeBlanc though he never carried their last name. He took pride carrying his mother's name and it confused the hell out of everyone else. The way his family had been fucking up since his Uncle Zalmon took the reins, it was better off not being associated with the now tainted brand.

Kedar, in fact, carried a dual citizenship. His mother was from New Zealand by way of Samoa. His father took her away from her people and everything that she knew. Life with him had not been easy, which was why she now resided in Hawaii. It was the one compromise she got from the divorce settlement.

She kept Kedar grounded, well, his mother and his grandmother – his father's mother. Rhoda Zelinka LeBlanc. The White Rose is what she was called. She really was a beautiful rose, but like a rose she also had thorns.

The misconception in the family structure for the LeBlanc's was that the world believed his arrogant uncle Zalmon and his simple assed son Vic managed Black Caesar International and all its subsidiaries, but those individuals within the family, knew how far removed that was from the truth. Neither of those idiots knew how many times they had been saved from death had it not been for either Zebulon or his grandson Z's interference. The White Rose was ruthless and pulled no punches when it came to business or family.

Rhoda LeBlanc or Grandma Rose as Kedar called her, was gifted. She was college educated with a Masters in Mathematics which made numbers and equations her love languages. Had computer programing been a part of her education, she would have owned the world. Instead, she settled for running one of the wealthiest families in the Caribbean. She did it with absolute class and echoes of mercy, just enough to let those that tried to push her remember what could have been.

Rhoda looked at Kedar now, with her glasses on the tip of her nose and smiled, "This little game you play – is it worth it?"

Kedar pulled up his phone looked at the picture he kept of Asa and exhaled with a sigh. As much as he wanted her, he knew this life would not be her right for her. While his name was clean, his family's – not so much. Asa was a delicate flower and though he could give her anything she desired. Kedar knew she was like the precious pottery she made, with too much water, or not cured long enough in the kiln, she would crack, and she was way too precious for that.

"She's a good girl Ma. Comes from a good family. Makes her own money. Has her own house. She's an artist. But most of all, she didn't deserve to be beaten like she was. He stomped on her like she was no more than an ant on the ground. That alone should have cost him his life. Let's not even talk about the fact that he was pimping out teenagers."

"Baby there are things in life worse than death. For the dying it's hopefully a momentary affliction, but for those that remain behind – hell on earth. Have you ever known the Zelinka's, or our foot soldiers to ever just straight out kill the offender?"

"No ma'am."

"Death for the wicked is the easy way. It really doesn't change the behavior of those still trying to get at you. The fear factor must be maximized making the lesson learned from the recipient a lesson that travels through the ethos whispered with fear and trembling from generation to generation. Find the weakness and tag it like a bee to its honey hive. Now are you going to try and court the young lady?"

And just like that the White Rose flipped 180. Unconsciously his lip twitched attempting to suppress the smile that was threating to take over his calm expression. His grandmother had a way of catching him flat footed. Clearing his throat to respond, Kedar wanted desperately to avoid the question. While he loved the White Rose beyond reason, his heart was his own affair. Besides they had bigger fish to fry. It was time, past time that Cass got his well-earned rewards. Part of that plan was underway. Nothing could ever replace the death of a child, but this would go a little way towards helping the family heal.

Looking at his grandmother with sympathy, "So what are you going to do about your grandson?"

"Don't try to dodge my question baby. If she is such a good girl, then why not put your feelings out there. You deserve happiness just like everyone else. You can't be a wallflower forever. Stop listening to your idiot father. Life is too short to live it in a box and you son, are just existing."

Pointing around the cabin of the plane, Rhoda continued, "You can't take any of this with you when you leave this world. Your father has money, but no purpose and a heart full of hatred. It's a miserable existence. Find that other part that makes you whole and it will go with you through space and time."

"So is Papa Z your other part," Kedar asked curiously.

"No. My first love was killed while serving in the military. Your Grandfather Zalmon Sr, and I started out as an arranged marriage between two modestly wealthy families. My family had the money and the talent but no foothold while his had the name and branding but were one financial quarter away from irrevocable ruin. It was sad really," Rhoda paused, shaking her head then continued. "Years of mismanagement was about to torpedo a company that had been in existence since the late 1700's."

Shrugging her shoulders at the memory, Rhoda went on. "To be honest I was heartbroken at the time and fighting depression. He was kind, patient, and helped me find balance, along with my own happiness. For that, I will always be grateful."

His grandmother looked away with a far-off look on her face. You could tell by her expression the memory was painful. One that even after all these years, the pain was still right there below the surface. It was a loss that Kedar couldn't comprehend because he'd never lost anyone that close. Kedar knew he wouldn't get this opportunity again, so he dove in headfirst.

"Is Zebulon Zelinka your son? Was your first love Zebulon's father?"

Though he didn't grow up in Barbados, he still kept up loosely with the family business. He knew the Zelinka's had a reputation for being a "business partner" that you called on when you wanted to decimate and leave no trace of whatever issues needed to be resolved. The polite term would be conflict resolution. They were as stealthy as the players from Assassins Creed and if you were in the life, you knew once the Zelinka's were brought in, so was the undertaker. Conversely, they possessed brains as well as brawn in their network. They were also evolving their reputation in the realm of cybersecurity.

Kedar needed a secure network set up at his home and he had heard the Zelinkas were the best. What he hadn't expected was the current head of the family, along with his successor, making a personal appearance.

When Kedar had met them at his front door, a few years ago he had been stunned speechless. Kedar and Z could pass for brothers and Kedar looked more like Zebulon than he did his own father, right down to the eyes, for sure they were related. He had known then that there was way more than his family was willing to tell. Once he got over the shock, Kedar and Z hit it off immediately and had remained close ever since.

Rhoda's head snapped around looking at her grandson carefully. "I'll answer that question with the understanding that there will be no more questions about this topic. Ever!" Rhoda paused at that moment to drive home the effect of her words. "That part of my life is sacred."

Nodding his head in understanding, Kedar waited for an answer. The answer he got he was not prepared for.

Removing the glasses from her face she looked at Kedar and said, "Your father and Zebulon share the same father. You are the spitting image of my first and only love. While your father has brown eyes, you my beautiful grandson, have eyes just like your grandfather."

Kedar sat back in his seat stunned. He had assumed he had gotten his eye color from his mother's people, but that was before he met Zebulon. That meeting with Zebulon and his grandson, Fernando, sparked an unquenchable fire that very few people could answer.

He, Kedar, was not a LeBlanc. He was actually a Zelinka.

"When your grandfather took one look at you after you were born, he knew. He knew there was no way in the world that your father, Edom, was of his blood. Unbeknownst to me, there was a DNA test performed to confirm his suspicion on both of his sons. It was then that he started to remove your dad from some of the business and basically changed his will so that only your uncle, his first-born son Zalmon Jr, would inherit any property." Rhoda shifted in her seat, agitated. Kedar could tell this was a conversation that still bothered her.

"Now what your grandfather couldn't touch was the trust that was set aside when your father was born. The only regret that I have is that neither your father nor your grandfather ever really did right by you. For that matter, none of the LeBlanc men did," Rhoda turned and faced the window with a distant mien, as long-ago memories seemed to assail her mind. "Instead of taking his anger out on me, your father blamed you, an innocent child. For that, I am so very sorry." She turned and looked at Kedar with love tinged with sadness and regret.

Life for Kedar growing up had been a living hell. By the time he was six his parent's divorce was final. Now he partly understood why. The constant arguments. The beatings he would get from his father for the least little infractions. Kedar spent many a night in his room dreading the time that his father would come home.

When his father fractured his arm, his mother packed what little she owned, and they left. Kedar later learned that when Rhoda found out what he had done to his own flesh and blood, she took it a step further and had both of his father's arms broken.

Since he liked to beat up on people, Rhoda deemed it only fair that she gave him an opponent worthy of a good brawl versus a five-year-old little boy. She put him in a boxing match and with an old sparring partner of Floyd Mayweather Senior who promptly whooped the wheels off Edom, making sure that both of his arms were broken along with several ribs when he finished. He couldn't even wipe his own ass for at least six weeks.

Kedar didn't find out about the boxing match until years later, but it made him love his White Rose even more. She truly watched out for both he and his mother when he was growing up. Coming to stay with them in Hawaii for a week in the fall and the winter. There was not a moment that went by that he didn't know how much she loved him. It was also Grandma Rose who made sure his mother had a handsome divorce settlement as well as wherever they lived, Kedar went to the best schools.

"Now as far as your cousin, you live by the sword you die by the sword. That dummy made his choice when he thought it was smart to skim from this family or worse pimp out little girls and boys! Out of all my grandchildren, Vic has had the greatest opportunity. He would have inherited the reigns because he initially showed promise, but he has no patience and apparently lacks morals."

Kedar didn't want to be on that side of the conversation when his grandmother talked to her Uncle Zalmon. Knowing his Grandma Rose, she already had what she needed. The conversation that they were going to have was going to lend him enough rope to hang himself. Some of this shit made sense now. Word on the street was that Uncle Zalmon was looking for wife number three. There was no way in hell he Zalmon Sr., the White Rose's husband and reigning patriarch would let anyone else, but his line inherits.
Grabbing his phone, Kedar sent a message to the man he could no doubt call his cousin, "Let the games begin."

Rhoda Zelinka-LeBlanc

The White Rose was always full of surprises, and she didn't disappoint when the plane landed in Charlotte. Rhoda had had her car shipped up from Florida and that's what was awaiting the traveling party at the airport once they landed. For the most part, she spent her time now between Barbados and Florida. Technically she had a dual citizenship. Although she had been born in the United States, her parents were not United States citizens – she'd squeaked in just before the government's rule change.

Her team was there at the airport grabbing her bags and giving her updates that couldn't wait. Akeem was there as well, informing Kedar of what had transpired with Nora. The meeting with Cass was set up to take place later that evening. Apparently, he grew a set and wanted to hold the exchange at one of the homes he believed no one knew about. Nora had done just as expected. Once she couldn't find her mother or her child, she turned to the one person she really trusted, her ex-husband. What kind of selfish bitch would do what she did to her ex-husband? There were so many things that in her selfishness she had stolen from him that he would never get back.

Rhoda turned to Kedar as if knowing what he was thinking. "Though I never agreed with the way your father treated you, I never kept your whereabouts from him. He could have called or visited to check on you, but his bitterness kept him away."
Kedar received what she said and filed it away for review later.

Every child should have the chance to interact with their mother or father until given a reason not to. For anyone to withhold a child from a parent out of pure selfishness was the lowest of the low in Kedar's opinion. Kedar just wished he could have been a fly on the wall when Nora broke the news to her ex-husband that she withheld the knowledge of a child, his child, all this time.

CHAPTER 2

Out of Time

Charlotte, North Carolina – Downtown

Slowing to a stop coming off the I-77 ramp to 5th Street, Peter Eriksson cracked his knuckles for the umpteenth time, so irritated at the prick he had to guard he had lost count. What he did know was he was roughly two knuckle cracks away from beating the wheels off Vic. Vic was playing Russian roulette with his life and mistakenly believed that he was untouchable. That asshole was ignorant and sadly mistaken if he believed his security detail was going take a bullet for him, not after the things that they had all seen. There is a code and somethings just were not done nor tolerated. Children were at the top of that list.

A tick started in Peter's jaw at the irony of his career choice. He who had served one of the most elite teams in the Marines was about to fail at the one thing he was an expert in, protection. Peter didn't blame himself though. Only a saint could take this level of irritation and such a man... he was not.

Peter pulled the overpriced SUV to the curb close to 1BAC. Downtown Charlotte was buzzing with activity. The city had changed much since he had last visited. Where 1BAC now sat was the old convention center. The old spot, now new and teeming with life, was the epicenter of activity including a new Ritz Carlton and a series of restaurants and bars.

"Pull behind Rhoda's SUV. We shouldn't be here long enough for you to require parking," Vic intoned distractedly, they would just follow Rhoda to whatever coffee shop she drove to.

Peter seethed in silence. That was the problem. Vic never paid attention to the things that counted. Like the fact, his Grandmother Rhoda's fleet had changed. If his eyes didn't deceive him, those were armor-plated trucks, military grade.

Hopping out of the driver's seat, Peter circled around the car, eyes searching for any possible threats to the White Rose. For her he would lay down his life, but for her grandson he would rather use him as a body shield. Looking at his charge he sucked his teeth in disgust. Vic was still distracted typing into his phone. By the time he realized his audience, it was too late.

Rhoda Elizabeth Zelinka LeBlanc would stand out anywhere. It was her height. She was easily six feet and insisted on wearing heels. Even in her late seventies, she still looked like a runway model. She kept her hair short and it was a beautiful iron gray. But with her heels on, Rhoda towered over Vic, and Vic hated that with a passion! He constantly complained that she never dressed her age.

Vic

Snapping his head up when the door opened, so that he could watch his footing as he stepped out of the car. Vic recognized for the first time something was off. Where there should have been a SUV, there were military like vehicles parked out front. Secondly and also belatedly, his Grandma Rhoda speaking with someone close to the entrance.

"Shit," Vic breathed harshly through his teeth. Mask in place and effecting an insouciant air, he walked up to his grandmother, the woman, and the child who should have been in his tender care as hostages. In an attempt to cover his shock, he straightened the invisible wrinkle in his suit jacket and moved forward, arms open as if he was going to embrace Rhoda. Instead, he was met with a full throaty laughter.

"Now now Invictus," holding up one finger and wagging it like a dog would with its tail, "You haven't hugged me since you were nine so let's not mess up a mutual understanding." Touché Vic thought.

She drew first blood. Taking a step back to cover his rejection and embarrassment, Vic took a moment to get a closer look at the lady and the little girl who stood beside Rhoda. The lady came to Rhoda's chin, but Rhoda did have on heels. It was one of the myriad things he hated about his grandmother. Rhoda was unusually tall for a woman, but for some ungodly reason, she felt the need to wear heels which always towered over his average 5'9.

Acting as if he wasn't even standing before her, Rhoda turned to her guest, "Hen? Go ahead and get the baby settled. I'll be there in a minute."

"Hen," as Rhoda called her looked at Vic with sympathy, gathered the little girl and walked to the SUV without a word. The security guard posted at the car opened the door smoothly, grabbing the young girl adeptly placing her in the car seat like he had done it every day.

Rhoda gained Vic's attention again when she spoke directly to his security guard. "Mr. Eriksson is it?"

"Yes ma'am," Eriksson responded more respectful than Vic had ever heard him sound. If Vic didn't know any better, he thought he saw a light blush go up the side of Eriksson's cheek.

"Heard about the work you've been putting in. You know we value loyalty at BCI, and I know your assignment has not been easy."

The last was said with an honest look of sympathy.

Eriksson cleared his throat and grimaced, "Ma'am you have some great folks on your staff."

"Now you're just being modest. I know the hell this boy put you through."
Vic almost dropped his phone but caught it in time before

responding, "Grandmother? Are you feeling okay? Do you need me to contact grandfather? You don't sound like yourself." Once again, his condescending, sickly sweet tone had Eriksson's hands clinching, unconsciously he cracked his neck. Rhoda stared at Eriksson intently, and he didn't break eye contact with her. He did his best to convey to her, silently, just how he felt. Rhoda nodded her head slightly confirming that she understood. His job was to be seen and not be heard; protect and not repeat. But no one wanted to protect Vic. Simply put, he was grimy, and no amount of money could wash away some sins.

Rhoda then turned her attention to her dimwitted grandson serving the same observant and calculating gaze. She was looking for some semblance of common sense. Anyone with an ounce of self-preservation could see the savage underneath all her beauty and chic groomed civility. "I'm perfectly fine." Once again, without missing a beat, Rhoda turned her full attention back to Eriksson.

"Thank you for your service and in a show of appreciation, we have decided to assign you to our South Pacific division. I know this is sudden, so we'll give you two weeks to get your affairs in order, paid of course," she smiled sincerely.

Raising his voice in an attempt to exert his authority, "You can't just reassign my staff. What is wrong with you? Have you lost your mind?"

At once her security moved forward, adjusting their suits, but Eriksson beat them to the mark. The body taps were quick and precise; one to the throat to stun and cut off his speech and the second to his mouth hard enough to make him bite his tongue.

Yelping like the hit dog he was, Vic bent over in shock at being touched and grabbed the handkerchief that was in his pocket. And just like the petulant child he's always been, Rhoda disregarded Vic and said to Eriksson, "Again, thank you for your service. You'll find your new assignment in the dash. You'll be reporting to my grandson, Kedar. Once you're settled, he'll get you up to speed on your duties."

Vic began to moan loudly, but neither paid him any attention as he struggled for breath while intermittently spitting out blood from his tongue bleed. Eriksson's prayers finally answered, responded truthfully, "It's been an honor working for you ma'am. Thank you so much for the recognition."

"My pleasure," Rhoda simpered eyeing the young man like he was a sweet piece of watermelon. "You can head out; Vic won't be needing your services for the rest of the day."

Nodding his head in thanks again, and without waiting for further conversation, Eriksson turned and did the bidding of his boss lady. For about three to five seconds he felt pity for the poor fool who was standing in front of one of the most beautiful, smartest, and deadliest people he had ever met. Rhoda Zelinka-LeBlanc was about to help her wayward grandson understand the meaning of mercy.

With no one between Rhoda and himself, Vic stepped closer into her personal space, mouth clenched attempting to whisper but his busted tongue wouldn't allow him, "Whaf is ong ith you? Way until my faver hears of thisssss!"

Rhoda burst out laughing, "Little boy, your father can't pass gas unless I give him the say so."

And just as pretty as you please, Rhoda deftly plucked the cell phone Vic was clutching like his life depended on it. Little did he know, it really did. "You won't be needing this where you're going."

With a snap of her fingers, Rhoda's detail came up, swiped his jacket back allowing Vic to see the weapon on his side, to let him know this was not a drill, and escorted Vic up to the first SUV.

While walking past, seething, the window rolled down and a smiling Kedar shook his head at his cousin and sucked his teeth, "You are one simple motherfucker!" To which Vic lunged at the window. Kedar didn't flinch, while on the passenger side, Z with his laptop chuckled at Vic's bitch-ass antics.

"Language!" Rhoda snapped the words, but her voice carried.

"My apologies grandmother," Kedar mumbled contritely, then blew a kiss at Vic.

"While he is simple you will not use that language around a lady. Understood?"

Kedar and Z intoned simultaneously, "Yes Ma'am."

She knew. How much she knew; Vic could only guess.
Vic was livid! He began to count down the grievances that he would report to his father. The first thing that Rhoda had done was strip him of his security detail. Next, she took his communication.

Lastly, she brought along his hated cousin Kedar. Whatever was going down it wasn't going to be good. The SUV had a raised partition between the rear seat and the driver, so he couldn't ask the guard what was happening, even if he wanted to.

It didn't take long for the thoughts in his head to start running possible theories together. But whatever she thought she had on him; his father would take care of it.

Of course, my father would take care of it. It's my word against a senile old woman. Took my phone like some kid she was putting on punishment.

It bothered Vic. What exactly did she know? And why was Kedar and the computer geek here? Oscillating between seething and panicking, Vic decided there was nothing he could do until they got to where Rhoda was taking him. Fear began to creep up his neck and his eye began to twitch. Surely his father would be there?

She'd better hope to God that Zalmon wasn't there, because as much as Vic tolerated his grandmother – to say he loved her was a bit strong, he didn't want to see his father take down her pride like only his father would.

Feeling more confident now that he had thought things through, Vic began to level out his breathing. He would just wait and watch. They were speeding down the interstate at a good clip. Vic saw a sign that said Cabarrus County and his stomach dropped.

Shit just got real.

Though Vic tried, communicating through the intercom to the security detail in the front, no one was talking so they just rode in silence. Looking behind in the window, Vic noticed the second SUV that contained Kedar split off and went to the right while his SUV kept straight on the parkway. When they'd passed by the road that lead to the Andino house, Vic almost shit a brick. This route was made with deliberation. His grandmother wanted him to panic.

Now it wasn't a matter of how much his grandmother knew, it was how much he could talk himself out of. Vic had tried to bribe the driver, but it was like talking to a brick wall. He had been isolated in a car without his security team and no form of communication.

The longer they rode, the more worried Vic became.
When they finally arrived, Vic smiled. He saw his father's men sitting outside the door of the lovely home that they pulled up to.

The door to the SUV was opened and Vic hopped out without a care in the world. Straightening his tie and still seething inside, but now gloating to himself that his grandmother was about to get her ass handed to her.

CHAPTER 3

Ascension to the Throne

Cassius
Cabarrus County

Cass sat on his deck overlooking the woods that surrounded his property. Out of all the properties he had amassed over the years, this one was his favorite. Located just off Trinity Church Road, there were only seven houses in the neighborhood, and each sat on a multi-acre lot. It was a gated community, complete with fencing, security, and custom-built homes.

Looking at his watch, Cass got up from his rocker and moved toward the front of the house. Kedar should be arriving at any moment. Like clockwork, the black SUVs began to roll into his circular driveway. Cass was ready to get this over with, but more importantly, he was ready to get his Nora back.

Drivers hopped out of the three cars and walked around almost in synchronization opening doors. Now this was money. Cass wasn't begging for bread, but he knew money when he saw it. What he didn't see, however, was Nora.

Opening the door to welcome his guest, Cass waited on Kedar to cross the threshold. Kedar walked in like he owned the place.

"My my my Cassius, somebody has been holding out." Kedar continued to walk into the house followed by four other men who were similar in looks and height. In fact, Kedar looked so much like one of the men who entered, he could have been his father.

As the remainder of the men who looked to be security, filed into the house – without Nora in their number – Cass became agitated.

"Kedar I have what you asked for. Now, where is Nora?" Ignoring Cass, Kedar continued walking around the interior randomly picking up artwork and nodding his head approving the work presented while the other men made themselves at home in his sitting room.

Lifting a piece that, on the market, would have cost roughly ten stacks, "Is this one of Asa's pieces?" Shocked that Kedar even knew who Asa was, Cassius didn't respond but rather watched Kedar resume his walk around the room like a perspective homebuyer. "The entire setup was weird," Cassius thought.

While Kedar roamed around the house aimlessly, the two men who looked to be related to Kedar made their way to the family room and made themselves comfortable. One man remained outside the front door, while three others made their way out onto the deck. They knew the layout of the house and were blocking all the exits. But how?

Cassius was trying to maintain his cool, but he was hanging on by a thread. He needed to see Nora, and Kedar was walking around like he was at an art show.

Without looking up, Kedar informed Cass, "You may want to check your front door," his voice reverberated off the foyer walls. Sure enough, three more SUVs pulled up into the drive. When the trucks stopped and doors opened and closed, Cassius knew the shit had just hit the fan.

As a beautiful older woman alighted from one of the vehicles, she approached the door and the man standing guard automatically stepped forward and proffered his hand, assisting her up the steps. She turned to Cass and smiled, "What a beautiful home you have Mr. Hewson."

Cass looked so confused yet responded courteously, "Th...Thank you, ma'am."

Vic entered the house and patted Cassius on the back, "Buck up

Buttercup. Everything's about to become clear."

Cass didn't trust any of these people, but he didn't have much choice. Looking out over his property, he could see men walking the perimeter of his property line. To the average person, it looked like he was having work done on the property, and the men in question were just mapping out the boundaries.

Cass understood the truth. Whatever was about to take place, there was no walking out the door and leaving. Taking one last look at the man on the porch, Cass slowly shut the door and made his way to the sitting room hoping against hope that someone could tell him what the hell was going on.

"The White Rose"

Cass felt like an antelope that had wandered into a lion's den. There were two factions in this room, the LeBlanc's… and everyone else. Cassius could only assume that the older man beside Mr. LeBlanc was his father, and Cass was clueless to the other people in the room with the exception of Kedar.

Tired of trying to guess what was going on under his own roof, Cass decided to cut to the chase, cleared his throat to speak, but the beautiful older lady in the room beat him to the punch.

Regally sitting in a wingback chair, she tilted her head up and to the side, taking in his measure, "Odd, you don't look like a pedophile." Cass sputtered trying to regain his composure from the verbal punch to his solar plexus she'd delivered with that statement and before he could recover, she turned her attention to the corner, "but then again looks can be deceiving isn't that right, Invictus? I mean, what else would you call a man who would not only pay for innocent, under aged, kidnapped children to be raped, but would also include those nasty mentally depraved, decrepit, and disgusting bastards you keep company with in your debauchery?"

Vic put his best mask on, hoping the silver tongue his delusional mind believed he possessed would work its magic on the crowd at hand, "Grandmother I have no idea what you're speaking of. I've met Cassius once or twice socially, but what he does on his personal time I couldn't tell you."

Turning to his father Vic continued to plead his case, "Father this is the exact thing I was trying to tell you." Looking at his grandmother with sympathy, "She's been confusing a lot of things lately." Speaking overly loud with the pretense that Rhoda had somehow lost her hearing, "Grandmother, maybe it's time you slow down some. You can't run forever. When's the last time that you've seen your doctor?"

Both Kedar and Z began to cough uncontrollably, but everyone could hear the suspicious sounds of laughing sprinkled liberally between the hacks, on the opposite side of the room until Rhoda gave them the eye. Both men straightened their ties and looked at the expensive hardwood flooring. Zebulon just rolled his eyes at the stupidity of it all.

Rhoda turned to Zalmon who came in the door right before she did – now sitting across from her, "My patience is thin, and we have other business to attend today."

Looking at his only son, Zalmon tried to tamper his slowly building anger and impatience. He knew that his son had a small side business, he didn't know about the prostitution and to add insult to injury the hookers were underage kidnapped kids. What was wrong with him? For his mother to make a personal appearance made this situation critical. He was months if not weeks away from taking over as CEO according to his father Zalmon Sr. Now with this issue, everything hung in the balance. Zalmon had not seen his mother this angry in a while. Frustrated that everything that he had worked for was now on the line because of this sniveling idiot. Zalmon stared at his only son. There would be hell to pay and it wouldn't be his blood that shed. The look was enough to make Vic clear his throat and find the nearest open chair.

"My apologies Mr. Hewson," Rhoda stood and walked over to the place where Cassius was standing. My name is Rhoda Zelinka LeBlanc. Some refer to me as the White Rose. More importantly, I'm the CEO of Black Caesar International, and the person that you have been in effect stealing money from for quite a while now."

Up close her beauty was mesmerizing which by itself made him dumbstruck. Her words just didn't make any sense. Cassius was flabbergasted taking it all in. He never took her money. Hell, he didn't even know who she was until she introduced herself. Ma'am, Cassius started off shakily, "I'm not sure what Kedar told you, but I promise you that I have never stolen money from you or your company.

"Ah," Rhoda sighed thoughtfully, "Invictus had you believing the money he invested into your little brothel was his?"
Hands on her hips, Rhoda quickly pivoted appearing to be in thought, walking back to the wing chair she was previously sitting in. Adjusting her dress to make sure that it appropriately covered her legs, Rhoda placed her elbows on the armrest of the chair hands steepled, index fingers pointing towards the soft curve of her chin.

"Fernando, can you run the tape please?"

"Yes ma'am!" Calling him Fernando threw Z off for a second. Only his beloved mother called him by his first name, and she was normally mad when she did. Snapping his fingers, one of the security guards moved to the center of the room and cracked open a laptop. Within minutes he had the laptop connected to a projector along with speakers and aimed at the only clear space on the wall.

"Mr. Hewson? You may want to take a seat." Rhoda intoned softly. Her subdued tone made everyone in the room slightly restless.

There he was, clear as day at what appeared to be one of Cass's after-hours spots. Vic was in the room overseeing the money count. The camera person did a panoramic circle around the room picking up everything and everyone from Cass, the guest along with the gambling tables. Vic's voice could be heard in the background asking how much his take for the night was, so far.

The cameraman then headed upstairs where you could hear the unwilling participants screaming and crying. At that point, the White Rose motioned to the security guard to pause the film. Vic still feeling like she had nothing on him and looking smug, he smiled, "Like I said Grandmother, Cass and I have run into each other at social gatherings."

Rhoda raised an eyebrow then smiled back at her idiot grandson and nodded to her security guard who went outside the door for a moment. When the trio of folks entered the room, both Cass and Vic knew they were not going to be able to talk themselves out of what would happen next.

CHAPTER 4

When it all Falls Down

"The White Rose"

Two men and what appeared to be a young teenager entered the room. Cassius knew who the young man was immediately. He was the one that had escaped from the house. If he recognized Cass, then he was screwed.

Rhoda stood looking at the men and requested, "Erik, thank you for your service to our family. Can you tell us if the man that paid for you and the other teenagers is in this room?"

Erik scowled and pointed to Cass, "He was the asshole who was in contact with Jamison and Sean. They had me in a room with some old pedophile that tried to rape me. After I let him beat my ass, I played dead. Once everyone was distracted, I hid in a downstairs closet until everyone left."

Pointing at Vic, "Him over there, was mainly watching the take. From what I was able to gather his take was about 70% of the proceeds. Considering this side business had been going for about two years at a gross of about seventeen million, let's just say that baby boy here has been robbing the family blind."

Vic roared and tried to come across the room at the young man but stopped in his tracks when his father boomed, "Sit your black ass down and carry this family name with pride while you still can." Looking at her grandson Invictus with loathing, "Does Erik look familiar? He should. His older brother drove you around for months. Both ex-military, Erik here takes after his mother. Small. Wiry. Met his mother while I was in college. Exchange student from Sweden. Do you understand how close knit as a family they are? I had to assure Erik's baby brother Peter on a weekly basis that you would be properly punished for your actions." The White Rose laid the facts out in a staccato fashion pausing briefly before each statement.

"Looks like you're not the only one with connections huh?" Kedar questioned with a look of disgust on his face.

Rhoda turned and walked over to a wingback chair sitting in the corner of the room. She sat quietly for a few moments deep in thought. Her eyes surveyed the room. They landed on two guards that were never far from her grandson's company. They looked about as jittery as dried corn over a hot stove. Once they left here today there would be only one matter of this particular business remaining. Ned and Harvey weren't the sharpest tools in the shed, but they chose to follow a dummy.

"Thank you, Erik, you may go." Rhoda looked at Kedar and asked,

"Are these the two men that wandered on to the Andino property and threatened Adelinda - Yes?"

A look of shock passed over Z's face because in his time with her, Del had never mentioned the intruders.

"Yes ma'am. That's what the security camera picked up," Kedar responded.

Hands steepled in front of her face, Rhoda's eyes shifted looking as cold as winter at the two men who because of their greed and stupidity, almost caused a blight on their family name. Something her grandson Invictus was never taught or just too dense to understand. Her money was on the latter.

"You work for me. You are paid by me. Yet you listened to this buffoon" using her thumb she pointed to Vic who had that stupid smirk on his face," The look on each of their faces was priceless. They looked at Vic hoping he would intervene stopping the train wreck that was sure to happen. They were disappointed. Vic wouldn't even make eye contact, too busy picking at the imaginary dirt under his nails.

"The simpleton who told you to trespass onto private property and assaulted this one's sweetheart," nodding her head towards her grandson Fernando. "A property of a family that we swore to protect. That has a beautiful set of twins that often run around in the yard," Rhoda ended softly almost thoughtfully.
Kedar looked at Fernando and raised an eyebrow mouthing at his cousin "sweetheart?"

Everyone turned to Fernando, who was trying to control his rage, but who everyone in the room should have been paying attention to, was Zebulon. Without saying a word, he walked up and shot both men in the head point blank. The shots were muffled by silencer, but the impact was just the same, especially to someone like Cassius who had never really seen death. Seeing those bodies drop quickly caused the smirk that Vic was rocking turn to a jaw drop.

"Shit," Cassius squealed involuntarily. He had spied the glint of the men's guns earlier and was trying to become invisible in the corner.

“Thank you, Zebulon. You know I detest loud noises. That takes care of one issue. Invictus? What do you think your punishment should be? You, a descendant of slaves that thought it was okay to use innocent children as sex slaves as long as it made a profit?”

“Grandmother I had no idea that he,” pointing at Cassius, “was hiring underage children. I never went into the rooms where they were located nor did I touch any of them I swear,” Vic tried to calmly explain.

“Ah, Invictus, but you still didn’t address the fact that you stole money from the family. Why did we waste tens of thousands of dollars sending you to the best colleges and universities? Don’t you have an MBA? Why do you think that I required all of my children and grandchildren to minor in accounting? Can you not read a balance sheet? I can – and quite often do!”
Kedar looked at Z and sneezed “Dumb ass.”

Vic’s nerves were on edge and he snapped, “Shut the fuck up Kedar! And why are you and the hired help here anyway?”
Singing sweetly, “Ah! Ah! Ah! Language young man!” It was the quite before the storm.

Looking at her poor excuse for a grandson, moments from slapping the taste out his mouth Rhoda’s temper was simmering just below the surface. “You have been around too many sycophants for far too long. You have forgotten who you are addressing and as such the respect that I not only deserve but what you will give, or I will be forced to snatch that lying sniveling tongue from your useless mouth!” Rhoda’s voice reverberated around the room like a clap of thunder because the entire room to become tense.

Erik appeared close to Rhoda’s side with a military grade serrated edge bowie knife. Vic knew in that moment if Rhoda felt so moved his tongue would be a thing of the past.

Glancing at Erik, Rhoda guffawed humorlessly, “My my you

really don't have any friends do you Invictus?"
It was then that Zebulon spoke for the first time when he looked at Zalmon and advised, "You need to get your son."

Zalmon sneered at Zebulon and addressed his mother, "Is there a reason why the Zelinkas are here? They have never been at the table before. Why now?"

"Great question my son! It is well past time that some wrongs in this family be righted. The only reason you are still breathing Zalmon and to a smaller extent Invictus is because I made Zebulon swear not to take your life after giving up everything that he loved to protect yours and you betrayed him."

Zalmon tried to act confused by his mother's statement but it was an epic failure. Rhoda knew her son better than he knew himself. "You knew that kindergarten dropout was taking money on the side. It was no secret; all the families knew yet you said nothing."
Kedar and Fernando looked at each other and mouthed,

"Kindergarten dropout?" Fernando added, "This shit makes so much sense now."

Kedar chimed, "Facts!"

"Probably has Mommy issues too," Fernando added thoughtfully, brow knit in examination of the things he was hearing.

"That would explain his lack of empathy for the treatment of those little girls held hostage under his care," Kedar appended on to the diagnosis of his cousin's phycological issues.

Patience running thin Rhoda slowly turned her head, looking at her grandchildren, lips purged.

Kedar familiar with his grandmother's facial expression looked at his cousin and jerked his head sharply conveying the signal to shut the next thought down.

Clearing his throat and looking sincere, "Sorry Ma."

Inhaling deeply now turning to look at her son and grandson Rhoda pointed her finger, "Help me understand why I would need to hear what my family members are doing from someone outside the family? Our business good or bad should never be made public. Do you know how embarrassing it was for me to get a call from Sadie St. Lucie telling me about my own family? Forget the fact that I already knew!"

At this point, Zalmon's face paled. None of the families were saints, but to be called out by another family for sloppiness spoke volumes as to how bad his son had fucked up, and by proxy himself as he knew what his son was doing and didn't stop him or inform his mother.
"Tradition states that the oldest should be next in line, but there is no way in this world or any other dimension I can deal with this level of incompetence. Kedar you will take lead on our U.S. obligations while Fernando will manage our International obligations. You two will start immediately.

Zalmon stood up so fast he knocked over the coffee table that was on the side of the chair. "Now wait a minute mother, you can't be serious! The Zelinka's are foot soldiers. They are not educated enough to run a major corporation!"

Zebulon had had enough and turned to confront the man who surely now knew the truth, but refused to recognize him for who he was, the oldest brother and rightful heir to his mother's throne.

"We were good enough to fuck, though weren't we?"

The rage, if it were visible would look like waterfall corralling down Zebulon's body in waves. Twenty plus years of frustration tempered by a mother's love and his vow not to strike finally freed. Zebulon had waited for this moment for a long time.

"All you had to do was make sure Isabell's bills were paid and that she was taken care of in my absence. Instead, you took advantage of her."

Zebulon thought of how his daughter suffered before he found her. Had it not been for the kindness of Earlene, only the Maker knows what would have happened? His sweet child suffered all because his self-entitled half-brother couldn't keep it in his pants. Even to this day, his daughter refuses to be in the same hemisphere as Zalmon, choosing to spend most of her time in Hawaii not far from Kedar's estate.

"Fucked her literally and figuratively, then shipped her and her unborn child off to die because you wanted to marry that dumbass's mother," Zebulon spat nodding in the direction of Vic. Zalmon walked across the room and went nose to nose with the man, Zebulon Zelinka, he would forever refuse to call brother. "What makes you madder huh? That I got to her first or that I was better?"

Zebulon pulled the weapon so fast Zalmon barely had a chance to react. Fernando ran across the room to try to reason with his grandfather, but Rhoda's voice calmed him first. "Son put down the gun. You are a Zelinka and we stand by our word."

Outwardly calm, Rhoda was breaking inside. There were so many scenarios that could have happened had not her granddaughter met the people she did. If she dwelled on what could have been, she would walk over to her son and slit his throat where he stood. It still would not erase the pain that her oldest child Zebulon was feeling at the betrayal. Besides, Rhoda knew firsthand that death was the easy way out. Living was so much harder. Rhoda wanted to make sure that Zalmon learned that lesson.

"You gave me your word that you would not kill your brother for his offense because he didn't know that he slept with his niece."

Cassius just sat in the corner watching the family drama play out and prayed that they wouldn't pay him any attention.

Zalmon stumbled back and looked like he had been god smacked.

Turning to his mother with a look of abject horror, he could only utter one word, "What?"

Rhoda rolled her eyes with impatience, "I don't know how to make this plainer. You slept with your niece, got her pregnant, and then shipped her to the United States. It took us years to locate her and that was only because of your son."

Vic piped up disagreeing, "I didn't know anything about this." Flabbergasted at the level of stupidity her gene pool possessed, Rhoda turned to the child who was both her great grandson and oldest grandson asking him to explain but Zebulon took the honor.

Zebulon still had his weapon aimed at his brother but had composed himself enough to speak, "All you had to do was keep her safe. Ten years. I gave up ten years of my life. Away from my family and everyone that I loved to cover up your sloppiness." He jabbed an accusing finger at Zalmon/Vic. "Your own father came to me and pledged that if I took the bid for you, my family would never have to worry about a thing for the rest of our lives. Your word is your bond. I didn't really trust your father, but I trusted my mother."

Zebulon slowly glanced at Rhoda then turned back to Zalmon.

"She begged me to take your place because she said, and I quote,

"He's too weak and they would break him in twenty-four hours.

He would end up making promises that he could not keep protecting himself and in the process doom not just our family but our entire network."

Zalmon still didn't believe what they were saying. She couldn't have been his niece. They were lying to get a rise out of him. Sensing that he was about to deny the truth again Rhoda held up her hand to silence him.

Rhoda looked at Zebulon, her firstborn son, with love in her eyes.

“I made a terrible mistake. I sacrificed the happiness of one son for the other, and I will have to live with that mistake for the rest of my life. What Zalmon did to my granddaughter I will take to my grave.”

The only other person Z was aware of that could talk his grandfather down was his mother. Z watched in awe as Rhoda, his grandmother and a woman he loved more and more with each passing day talk his grandfather down. Vic was confused, head bouncing back and forth between his father and Zebulon Zelinka but then his grandmother elaborated and made everything clear.

“That’s why I’m naming your grandson,” Rhoda announced, clutching Zebulon’s arm, “and your son,” she turned looking at Zalmon, “part heir of the corporation. It is clear to me Zalmon, that even after all the chances and opportunities afforded to you both,” she turned looking at Vic, “you two would have our family exposed and broke within a year of running it.”

Regaining his voice, face mottled in outrage, Zalmon looked as if he was about to swing on his own mother, and he began shouting.

“Mother you have lost your fucking mind if you think that I’m handing my legacy over to this bastard. I don’t even know if the little fucker is mine!”

Walking up to her son, Rhoda swung from the shoelaces, smacking the taste out of her son’s mouth.

“Don’t you ever curse at me again! Do you understand me? The next time I won’t stop your brother from putting a bullet in your head. I run this family! Me! When I had your brother, I wasn’t married. He took my maiden name. Do you know what that means?”

Zalmon actually clenched in fear. His mother was a Zelinka. The Zelinkas were the boogie men of the Caribbean. No one crossed one and survived. Vic tried to pipe up but one look from his father silenced him.

"Now, Mr. Hewson," Rhoda turned to Cassius, calm and collected, as though she didn't have a care in the world, "you had no clue that my grandson was stealing from the family, but you" she evinced pointing directly at Cassius, deliberately punctuating the 'you' "put a wonderful young lady in the hospital, over a ring that you stole.

Plus… well, anyone who would solicit young children, deserves to go to prison."

Cass was too scared to say anything, so he just sat there. He didn't want to end up like the two men on the floor.

"You will, however, do one thing for me." Rhoda snapped her fingers and a man was ushered in the door while a few of her men came in with plastic and cleaning supplies.

The men immediately walked over to the two bodies on the floor and started stripping them. One man walked over to Rhoda with a briefcase in his hand. Cass noticed that one of the dead men had a bad bite mark on his leg. Something had bitten the hell out of him.

He had been so fixated on what the men wrapping up and removing the bodies were doing, he'd almost missed what was being said.

"I'm sure you would concur that it is only appropriate that the families of your victims which you've irrevocably destroyed, by abducting their children deserve to be compensated? Wouldn't you agree?"

Cass would agree to anything at this point to leave this house alive and not wrapped in plastic. Rhoda looked over at her grandsons,

"What did you say he had hidden at the other houses that he owns?"

Kedar answered without looking up from his phone, "Roughly

eleven million, give or take. Mostly in gold and silver bars. In his bank accounts, he has about one hundred thousand, liquid."

"Fernando dear? Could you make sure that the money we discovered in the houses is divided up amongst the victims as well as Asa Altman and the Andino family for the injury and the break in on their property."

"Grandma, you can call me Z. The only person who calls me Fernando is my mother… when she's angry with me," he chuckled making his way over to the laptop that was on the table.

She smiled indulgently and murmured, "I'll try to remember that baby. Now the houses are another matter. I have the titles here and I'll need you to sign. My assistant here is a notary. This house will be given to little Fiona. Do you know that your accomplice Sean attempted to strangle her to death on the Andinos' property?" Rhoda had made it her business to get updates on all the living victims that she could find. All of them tugged at her heart because they did not deserve any of the things that happened to them.

"Her family needs a place where they can stretch out and live comfortably after all they've suffered. Little Fiona will also need round the clock care until she comes out of the coma." She turned her attention back to her assistant, "The remainder of the houses will be sold at market value. Have it funneled through one of our family charitable funds. Inform the families that you are working on behalf of Mr. Hewson and he wants to reconcile his wrongs.

While it will never be enough to repay what he played a hand in, it will be a starter."

Facing Cassius, "You will also make restitution to Ms. Elliot. The house you destroyed where, yet another little girl died. She drowned trying to escape the hell you and your business partners had trapped her in."

"Ma'am I didn't kidnap any girls. That was all my cousin, Jamison. I had no idea where he was getting the girls from," Cass pleaded.

“So, you concede you did know that the young ladies were there not of their own volition?”

Too late did Cassius realize the trap he’d unwittingly walked into. Scrambling trying to find a logical denial of what he’d freely admitted was true, Rhoda spared him the effort, “You know Mr. Hewson I had a dossier created for you. I have one on everyone under my employ.”

“Ms. LeBlanc, I swear to you that I did not know that your grandson Invictus was stealing money from your company,” Cassius pleaded fervently.

“Which I find plausible, but still not excusable considering your stellar business acumen.” The last was stated with clearly detestable frown.

Studying him visibly, Cassius felt as if he were sitting down for a job interview and the benefits were either life or death. “I read your file. College graduate. Great promise when you first started in the business world until you became too attached to monies that weren’t yours. Your mother to the rescue because she believed in your innocence and your father because he would not let the family name be tarnished. Something as a mother and a CEO I can empathize with,” switching her attention over to her son Zalmon and his son and prodigy Invictus. Her eyes said it all. She was not pleased. Zalmon adjusted his body in the chair. Rhoda knew his mind was spinning trying to come up with a bonafide excuse, complete with a disaster recovery plan.

Rhoda focused her attention back to the subject at hand. “The problem is you never learned. So, you kept doing things that drove you further and further away from morality. Stealing a few items here. Shaving a few numbers there to skim off your parent’s business. As long as no one was hurt what did it matter?”

“Ms. LeBlanc I am a businessman. I swear to you that I was only trying to uphold a business offer that your grandson Invictus presented."

She may have been pushing three score and ten, but this younger generation somehow thought that age made you senile or made you forget all the lessons and things you learned along the way which was preposterous. No still meant no in any language or at any time – whether it was 1960 or 2020. "So, you believed all those young girls came to your establishment willingly?"

"Well, honestly I didn't think about it. Maybe not all of them… no ma'am, not all of them," Cassius stuttered belatedly realizing his mistake. Eyes wide and flashing, he tried to correct his mistake. Before he could speak the White Rose was on him once again.

"Any good business owner is going to know his goods and services from the vendor to the warehouse floor. You monitor to make sure that there are no defects or flaws that would cause your customers to lose faith in your ability to deliver."

Using her index finger, Rhoda tapped a rhythmic beat, thoughts marching arranging the sickening logistics in her mind getting angrier by the second at what those poor young men and women suffered.

"You stood there and watched those young girls being sold like cattle at an auction without an ounce of compassion. Watched them cry and shrivel, yet you stood there and did nothing." Driving her final point home, Rhoda's voice became louder and more punctuated with each sentence.

"No, you didn't snatch these poor innocents from their homes, you let your cousin do the dirty work. You somehow convinced yourself, more than likely encouraged by the swelling bottom line you and that," motioning her thumb over her shoulder at her grandson Invictus, "sorry excuse for a man thought it was okay to enslave children for sex. While you didn't physically remove them from the safety of their homes and families, you didn't send them back nor did you turn down their services," Rhoda said coldly.

Misunderstanding what Rhoda meant, Cassius tried again this time almost screaming in his angst to get her to see his side and show mercy, “I NEVER SLEPT WITH LITTLE GIRLS!”

“No, you just handed young girls who barely knew themselves let alone their own bodies to old depraved men, doing things to them that their minds were ill-prepared for. Did you not see the fear in their faces when they were brought in? No? Riiiiiiight you were too busy counting the money you were making off their bodies,”

Rhoda said pressing her point. “Do you know what it feels like to be taken against your will? No? You'll be learning soon.” Turning to her grandson, “Z make sure some of those dollars go to local charities that deal with rape victims and missing children.” Snapping her fingers and pointing to his abdomen, “My men are going to take you to a friend of mine who has a going away gift for you. Once you receive it you are free to go. I'm not going to tell you what to do, but I would advise you to make the most of the time that you have remaining. Because of the young lady found floating right on the banks of the property, your family is already under investigation. You have about twenty-four to forty-eight hours before the Kannapolis City police catch up with you. Just know that if you are caught on any Zelinka, LeBlanc or Andino property you are to be killed on sight. You know what? Let's add the Altman's to that list.”

“Well I think I'm done here,” Rhoda said cheerily to the room at large as if she hadn't just pronounced a death sentence on someone. “How are we looking Fernan – Z?”

“Done. Just looking at some comps on the property. This one should go for at least a million easily. Good thing he had hardwood in here because getting those blood stains out of carpet would have been a bih – I mean very laborious,” Z smiled catching is misstep in time. The last thing he wanted today was get on his grandmother's bad side.”

In his delusional mind, Cassius believed that while he may go to jail, it would only be brief. That girl could have come from anywhere. Besides, there was no way in the world his mother would let him stay any length of time in jail. She'd mortgage the family home first, with or without his father's permission. Besides, they still didn't have all his cash. He still had gold coins hidden in a wall safe at his parent's house. FOCUS! He screamed internally.

He needed to move to survival mode. What to do???? He just needed to make sure that Nora was safe. Once he got out on bail, he could explain everything, and they would fight the charges together. He could do twenty-four hours in county. He did it before and he'd do it again. Gathering his voice while wading through fear he asked, "What about Nora? Is she safe?"

Kedar looked up from his phone and frowned. While Z was working on the comps all the properties, Kedar was being obedient and wiring funds to the local charities that his grandmother requested. "Exactly how obtuse are you? Let me try to break this down for your tiny mind. Vic – your partner over there was going to hold both Nora's little girl and her mother hostage. You didn't even know Nora had a child! She never trusted you with such sacred information. You were just a means to a bag. You would have never been able to get out of the trap he's set. You are working with hundreds of thousands, just barely breaking millions while he operates in billions. How did you think this would play out?" Kedar asked, genuinely curious about Cass's answer. He could see the wheels finally beginning to turn albeit fatalistically late.

"What? Leaving? Was that your next move? That you could just leave? What were you going to do? Run from place to place, state to state? You were never going to be able to take Nora around the world like you dreamed. Once she found out who you really are and what you did, she never would have stayed with you. As greedy as she is, she cherishes her daughter more than anything and you handed that idiot" he nodded toward Vic, "the keys to crush her world."

Kedar turned away from the two jackasses and spun his attention to his Grandmother.

“I think the rule needs to apply to Nora and her family as well. That little girl shouldn’t suffer because of her mother’s poor taste in men.”

Rhoda nodded, “Done. And not because of the mother, but the fact that that little girl’s grandmother has done things for me as a friend that could never be repaid.”

Rhoda’s face had a distant look on her face like she was trapped in time. She suddenly shook her head as if she was struggling to come back.

Belatedly realizing exactly how trapped he was, Cassius stood running his hands through his head ripping at the strands mumbling softly at first, “No, No. This can’t be happening.”

“Oh, and Invictus? Zalmon?” Rhoda pressed, “As of yesterday you two are stripped from all family account access and properties.

You are officially on your own dime until I choose otherwise. I’m sure the nest egg you’ve collected will help. That little board you started with your peers to give unsanctioned shipping contracts at discounted rates is squashed as well. The money you accepted, returned.”

Cassius oblivious to the words being spoken around him went into full freak-out mode, “Please Ms. Leblanc you have to believe me. I was a victim in all this! This is not my fault. I would never hurt anyone purposely! You have to believe me!”

Past the point of caring about civility and decorum, The White Rose unleashed her true thoughts, “Like when you beat that poor Asa, kicking – even stomping her over and over until she passed out? The same girl that you because of your “non-violent ways” had to go into physical therapy due to the wounds you inflicted. Or maybe it was the loan on Asa’s house, which was tied to family property by the way that you allowed to go into foreclosure not because you didn’t have the money – simply because you simply didn't give a damn."

Eyes glowing with the power of her anger Rhoda pressed her last point home, "Every night when you try to lay, you're head down to rest in the next several weeks and years to come and you hear that sound? The sound of some malicious, perverted prisoner creeping into your cell who corners you along with anyone else who loves fresh meat and takes your little weak frail body placing it ass up and face down, I want you to repeat the same – that you're just a victim in all this."

Standing and walking over to him face to face, "Now gather yourself!" Cassius's response was to do the exact opposite collapsing to the floor, clutching his knees and rocking in desperation.
With a snap of her fingers, Rhoda's assistant appeared by her side with his notary seal and pre-printed documents. One of the guards slide a table right in front of the place where Cassius was rocking. The pages were already highlighted and marked. Sniveling and snorting, Cassius shakily reached for the pen that was placed in front of him, breathing heavily, tears falling while signing his life away.

CHAPTER 5

Checks and Balances

"Gentlemen once Cassius finishes signing the papers, our business here is complete," Rhoda made the statement so casually you wouldn't think she'd just crushed the dreams of three grown men. Rhoda's team moved like a well-oiled machine, moving bodies and cleaning evidence while she sorted out family business between her misguided grandson Vic and his pretend clueless father. Cassius was busy signing his life away with an occasional snort and nose wipe.

Rhoda looking for some sense of remorse posed, "Mr. Hewson? This act of kindness should make you feel a wee bit better right?" It was really a closed end question. No amount of money could erase the pain that Cassius and her idiot grandson Invictus had caused. At least the house was never used for gambling or prostitution. Rhoda looked around noting the pricy fixtures, "I take it this was your personal residence?"

Rhoda snapped her fingers just as Cassius finished signing the last document, causing him to fearfully rise up dropping the pen to the floor. "Yes ma'am," he answered carefully, his voice was shaky with fear. Rhoda smirked in no attempt to facially hide exactly how she felt. Cassius was trying his best to sound calm and considering the dead bodies being rolled out of what was his home in boxes. It was wise on his behalf not to end up as another body for her men to clean up. Good.

"Time to go. If you try to contact your cousin, Jamison, once you are out of my tender care… well let's just say, you wouldn't like it."

Cassius nodded too afraid to speak. He had the keys to this house in his pocket but felt that he would never see the house again. Following Rhoda LeBlanc also known as the White Rose out of his beautiful home, Cassius just hoped they would allow him to turn himself in.

Once they were assured that all signatures were in place, the bodies had been removed, and the floor had been cleaned. Zebulon, Z, and Kedar made their exit out of the house without another word. Rhoda would send a crew back later to clean the house from top to bottom before she delivered the keys to Fiona's family.

The last to leave the house were Zalmon and his son, Vic. No words were spoken because they had just gotten schooled by, who they thought was, a doddering old lady. Both men were in their minds thinking this was not the end, but both were also too dumb to see that their mother and grandmother – in her own brutal way –

had just saved their lives.

One thing did bother Vic, though, out of all the things that had gone down. Where was Akeem? Kedar and Akeem, those two were never far apart. Akeem was Kedar's fixer. Any small details were always ticked and tied by Akeem. If he was not present, then someone was either dead or dying.

Zalmon shook himself out of his stupor and walked over to the SUV his mother and her elite security were walking towards.

"Mother? A moment please?" Normally business like and brusque at best, Zalmon unknowingly showed the range of emotions that flowed across his face. "You can't be serious?"

Carefully sliding into the plush leather seats of the SUV, the door was closed by her security and the window slowly rolled down. Rhoda took her time adjusting her dress before addressing her second oldest son. "As serious as the money you and your son stole from the company."

Reaching out her left hand to her assistant who firmly placed a small piece of paper in her hand. "You have one week to have the amount of money in my account."

Taking the paper into his hand, Zalmon reached into his pocket and grabbed his reading glasses. Spine straightening, he stepped back and stumbled baffled by the numbers written.

"Mother this number can't be right!"

"Let me see that please." Quickly handing the paper back to his mother, Zalmon was positive that a mistake was made.
Rhoda looked at the number briefly and handed it back to her assistant looking at her son, "I stand corrected." She then handed him another paper.

"Every time you question me or my authority that number will increase twenty-five percent. Now care to tell me that I'm wrong again?"

Sweat now beaded on Zalmon's brow. He didn't have that kind of capitol on his own and neither did his son. Watching her son Zalmon closely, Rhoda waited on a response.

"No ma'am," forcefully spewed from Zalmon's lips.

"I thought not," Rhoda intoned with a smile. "Now we both know your next play. You'll run to your father and tell him that I'm not being reasonable. You'll run to your baby brother and try to convince him that I need to be removed from the board. If you have not figured it out by now son, there is nowhere to run to that I have not already covered. You may still have some lingering doubts about who actually runs this family, but in the words of the illustrious sweet crooning James Brown – Try me!"

Tight lip and mind spinning trying to figure out how he would come up with outrageous amount his mother was demanding, Zalmon could only stand there staring at the woman he believed was past her prime and needed to retire.

"Now as this young generation says," turning to look at her assistant. Zalmon couldn't hear what was said but Rhoda made it clear, "Run me my money!"

Saying all that she intended to say to her son for now, Rhoda Zelinka LeBlanc also known as the White Rose rolled up her window and the sophisticated armor-plated SUV followed by two other SUVs rolled out of the drive.

Zalmon watched as the armored SUV pulled slowly out of the drive and on to the main road. He could hear footsteps moving behind him, but it was all muffled and secondary. He just couldn't get past the stupidity of his son. The more he thought the madder he became. Yeah, he knew that his son had a few irons in the fire, but he had no clue that the dumbass was running a child trafficking ring. None of them were saints by a longshot, but children? He thought it was okay to traffic children?

"Father, I swear to you I didn't know that Cassius was bringing in underaged girls."

Zalmon watched his son and listened to the lying words roll off his tongue so easily. If he lied about this, then what other information was he withholding? Walking up to his son he decided to set the table so that it would be clear exactly how the menu would be going forward.

With his security surrounding him, surveying the property for any threats, it was ironic that the threat to his survival was not from the outside, but from his own seed. True to her word, his mother had stripped Invictus of everything, right down to his security detail. His son was down to what he came into this world with, nothing.

As he approached his son, self-preservation belatedly began to seep into his tiny brain. Vic backed up a step, bumping right into a column that held the light shining on the circular bend on the beautifully stoned driveway. Hand extended, grabbing his second oldest son, wrapping his palm around the back of his neck. Today was one full of revelations. Once he had time to cool his anger, he would reexamine his oldest son, but for now he had more pressing matters.

"Father…" his son tried again to talk his way out of what they both knew at this point was a lie.

Trying to calm himself before he did something that he couldn't take back, Zalmon tried to start off calmly, "Son, while we may lie to the world, we never under any circumstances lie to each other." Vic was trying to maintain his composure but losing the battle. Very few people could break him, and his father was one of them. Too nervous for words, he nodded his head.

"Now what else do I need to know about your failed venture?" Vic cleared his throat. The fact that his father had not let go of his neck ratcheted up his heartbeat just a little. They were never touchy feely, so this was uncomfortable to the extreme.

"I only dealt with Cassius and his cousin Jamison, but mostly just Cassius," he stuttered.

Nodding his head in encouragement, Vic continued at his father's direction.

"Jamison and his partner Sean were trying to get on with us fulltime and had applied at our offices in Charleston."

"And where are these gentlemen now?"
Vic stared at his dad with fear in his eyes, but this was not something he could hide.

"Sean was killed on the Andino property by Fernando's bitch, I mean girlfriend," quickly covering his mistake of cussing.

A confused look passed over Zalmon's face, "Why did she shoot him?"

"Because he was choking out a girl on the property."
Zalmon blinked rapidly looking to the left, then to the right, then back at his son. The cesspool was deeper than he imagined. How in the world did he get here? This entire situation was a death trap and his son in his greedy ignorance was leading the charge. How could he be dumb enough to believe that his mother didn't know all of this? It was then that the same blood that flowed through his mother's veins pulsed hard and he snapped.

Changing the position of his hand from the nape of Vic's neck to the front, Zalmon began to squeeze. No words were said, he just tried his best to get his thumb and index finger to touch. Vic's feet kicked wildly. The security team stood back and watched dispassionately. They were to be seen and not heard and sadly enough no one cared enough about Vic to intervene.

"Faath, Faath," Vic weakly strangled out. He clutched at his father's hands trying to get him to release his grip.

"You were given everything. Everything!" The last was said with a scream.

"How can you be this stupid? She has stripped us of everything! WE HAVE NOTHING!"

"Ple…" Vic tried again to plead with his father for mercy. Zalmon was unmoved. His mind was spinning. His poor excuse for a son almost destroyed access to billions over millions. His mother was right, mistakes like this made Vic unqualified to run the family business, but why should he be punished for his son's incompetence? It was time for plan B.

Abruptly he released his son, turning his back and pacing away not even watching as he collapsed in a heap to the ground.

Rubbing his hand through his long neatly locked hair, Zalmon tried to compose himself. He never let that side of him come out, but in this case, it was warranted. That boy needed to understand that this wasn't a drill and every action had a reaction.

Randomly a thought entered his mind as he combed through his mane trying to center himself. Fernando's hair is just as long as mine. If what Zebulon said was true and Fernando was in fact his son, then the boy did well.

Breaking from the thoughts he was not ready to deal with, Zalmon watched as Vic still struggled to breathe sitting haphazardly on the ground, "Do not call your grandfather. I will handle that conversation."

Coughing up a lung Vic managed to get out, "Yes Sir."
"As a matter of fact, don't do or say anything else until I give you permission."

Nodding to his security, one of the men walked over and picked Vic off the ground.

"Take him to his mother's house."

Zalmon began to walk towards his SUV that was now quietly pulling up to the curb.

“Make sure that he is guarded at all times. No more mistakes!”

“Invictus? His father asked, “That fact you still breathe right now is the last blessing that I pass on to you. If I find additional items that were not revealed today by the time, I return to your mother’s house… Let’s just say you better have your affairs in order.” With that said, Zalmon Invictus the second slipped into his awaiting vehicle and drove off into the night.

***

Days later after he had got his affairs in order, Cassius did in fact turn himself in and sang his swan song better than a Grammy hopeful. His performance – spectacular. He was forced to run the illegal gambling house by his cousin Jamison Hewson. If it was believed, Cassius claimed that his cousin Jamison threatened his life and demanded the properties be used. Jamison provided the girls and the clients and all he did was open the house. While they booked Cassius on a myriad of charges, it was too neatly tied together but the bosses wanted closure, so Ed and Rohan had little choice in closing out the case with the two folks they had in custody.

CHAPTER 6

Stay Woke

Jamison Hewson

Punching the button for the garage on the remote, Jamison Hewson pulled into his new home to park in the garage, so he could get the few bits of groceries out of the car. He had about another week here then he'd be Charleston bound to begin his new job at the port. The world as he knew it was about to change for the better. Invictus LeBlanc had all but guaranteed it. Too bad his boy Sean wouldn't be around to celebrate their newfound wealth, but to the victor goes the spoils. So, preoccupied with how he was about to spend this bank he was sitting on, it took him a moment to recognize something was off. Something wasn't right, but he couldn't put his finger on it. The house smelled… earthy?

Dropping the bags on the table, Jay froze where he stood. They were sitting on the couch as if they had been watching TV when it happened. There was blood on the couch where the heads were resting. Jay didn't look at the scene long, he immediately pivoted and ran down the hall to grab his things from the bedroom. Shit, he thought. He'd have to make two trips. Dipping into the bathroom, Jay went to the closet and tapped hard on the left side of the wall.

The sheetrock pulled away and Jay grabbed the bag he had hidden. Not bothering to shut the door Jay turned and ran right into a hard-left hook. Akeem stood over him expressionless but spoke like he was Jay's long-lost friend.

"Thank you for getting the money out of hiding. We didn't want to tear up the house looking for what we knew you'd lead us straight to."

Shaking his head trying to remain awake and think at the same time Jay blurted, "Who the hell are you?" even though it didn't matter.

Another man stepped into his line of sight but said nothing. Von, was the other man's name. He worked for the White Rose and wanted to be there when they caught the sick sons of bitches that were stealing kids. This genius deserved what anybody who messed with kids got. All he could think about was when he'd watched that precious little girl and her grandmother running and playing in the park. Shaking his head in anger, Von wordlessly walked out of the bathroom.

Jay tried to pull himself up off the floor, but Akeem's boot pushed his head back down. The punch had been so strong it'd left Jay struggling to stay awake. Jay wasn't sure how much time passed but the man who had been in the doorway came back with a metal stick with what looked like an emblem on the end. The stick was glowing red and orange like it had been stuck in… fire? Still groggy and weak, Jay tried to fight but the quiet man flipped him over, effectively trapping his arms while the other man restrained his legs and pulled his pants down. Jay began to struggle in earnest at this point, afraid of what the man was going to do next.

Jay could feel the heat drawing close to his body and began screaming. The brand was placed on the left cheek then on the right. The smell of flesh, his flesh, burning and the pain was so intense, Jay was on the verge of losing consciousness, but before his eyes closed, he heard the man who'd inflicted so much pain as he regarded his handiwork, "At least his cousin can get his removed. This shit right here will last a lifetime. Ain't no coming back from that."

Akeem nodded then took the gun that had been given to him by Zebulon Zelinka, scrubbed it down of prints, and placed it in Jay's limp hand, making sure he gripped it. He pulled Jay's pants up, hiding the fresh burn marks.

Retrieving a burner phone from his pocket, Von dialed 911 and reported that he had heard shots fired and someone needed to get to this address immediately. They left as quiet as they'd come and made their way to the parked black SUV down the street. They were assigned with making sure Jamison Hewson never enjoyed freedom again.

Adelinda

Adelinda Marie Esparza sat on her deck facing the woods and watched nature awaken in the early morning sun. Steam wafted from her cup of coffee and she realized she had something that she had not experienced in a very long time. Peace. Lifting the elixir of life to her now smiling but parted lips, Del blew across the surface, breaking the tension and took a tentative sip. Nirvana.

While her mood was indeed peaceful what should have freaked her out was the assortment of wolves scattering her lawn. They lounged in various spots and looked to be sleeping but Del wasn't fooled. At the least sign of trouble, they would be up and alert. Ezra, the owner and caretaker of these beautiful creatures, and Del had been bantering back and forth since the first time that she laid eyes on them. Ezra swears they are Kugsha, but no one believed that tall tale. Her best friend Charleston, who was a vet, said that the hounds were something much older and shouldn't be alive, dire wolves.

How Ezra was able to obtain and keep alive a breed of canine that should have been extinct thousands of years ago was anyone's guess. All that mattered to Del was that she considered them her friends and was damn glad that they considered her one as well.

Luke, nearly pure black in color with the exception of the diamond on his chest, made his way up the stairs and unceremoniously plopped right beside Del, nuzzling her hand that was absently hanging off the side of the rocking chair she was occupying.

Luke was the name that she had given him because he reminded her of her favorite comic book character, Luke Cage. And just like Luke Cage he was a bad mutha sucker in a fight. Staring down at her unlikely friend, Del smirked, "Think it will stay quiet around here?"

Luke leaned his ginormous head back, canines flashing in a slight doggy grin and let out a howl. The listless pack that was laxed and lounging snapped to attention, sat up, heads tilted towards the waning moon and joined in adding their baleful voices to Luke's. It was both beautiful and daunting at the same time.
Smile dropping from Del's face, she looked out over the property and sighed. Lifting her cup, she took another swig savoring the taste and thought aloud, "Maybe I should have just stayed in Afghanistan. I think I would have been safer." As if understanding

her thoughts, Luke stopped mid howl and gazed at his friend with an expression of confirmation.

Her phone, which was never far alerted her to a text message. Picking it up Del read the bold text message, "Are you packed yet?"

Sighing heavily, Del's head slumped forward chin to chest. Z was relentless. Once he had something in his mind, it was a done deal.

Luke nudged her hand gently standing to his almost four feet in height. Looking at her sometime companion, she called bullshit. Shaking her head and laughing. There was no way in hell something that big should be alive in this century, for sure they were pre-historic. How they were in her yard now was a mystery that made her head hurt and right now she had bigger fish to fry.

Del could she a set of eyes shining like diamonds from the woods and she knew that her company would be dispersing. Recognizing their alpha's authority, the pack stood, stretching shaking their huge heads and sporadically started moving towards the woods that surrounded the house. She never joined them, but she was always near.

"Good Morning," Del called out across the lawn. As if in greeting, she dipped her regal head, turned and moved back into the shadows.

Looking at Luke Del intoned conspiratorially, "I don't think she likes me."

Feeling compassion for his friend, Luke again nudged his muzzle against her palm, crossing in front of her chair, he leaned against her leg. The weight of his body causing the chair to grown just a little. Placing both her now empty coffee cup on the table along with her phone, Del reached out and rubbed Luke's flank with both hands.

"Off you go now! You don't want to keep her waiting."

Positioning his head into her palm, Luke licked it gently then turned, lunging off the porch in one leap. At the edge of the woods, he looked back one last time before disappearing into the morning mist.

Yard now empty, Del stood stretching and grabbed her cup and her phone. If she was going to give this relationship a chance, she had to play fair. Heading to the house, she wondered if she should pack knives as well. She never left home without her weapons, and she wasn't about to start now. Luckily for her she wouldn't have to go through TSA to board the flight she was about to take.

Cassius

Though he turned himself in at the Kannapolis Police Station, he was transported and processed at the Mecklenburg County Jail in downtown Charlotte. After he got off the van, he and a group of prisoners were taken into the arraignment room to see the magistrate so the formal charges could be received. It was a slow night, so Cassius didn't have to wait long.

"All rise," the bailiff spoke crisply, voice resonating all over the room.
Cassius waited patiently, curious on who his mother would send to help him defend the charges. She actually went with him when he turned himself in, assuring him that everything would be just fine and not to worry.

"Hear ye! Hear ye! The honorable Sibbie Juanita Grissom is now presiding."

A small African-American woman robbed in black took the bench with a polite smile on her face. Surveying the courtroom briefly Judge Grissom responded sternly, "You may be seated."

The District Attorneys and other counsel were now moving somewhat freely around the bench addressing the clerks who were organizing stack of dockets that would be processed in the next several hours.

Cassius looked around the room hoping to find a spark of recognition from one of the well-dressed attorneys. Surely one of them would be handling the charges. At least five minutes had passed, and no one had called his name to match him up with any of the lawyer's present. Panic begin to set in. He gave his mother the money with strict instructions on who to contact.
The bailiff came forward once again, "Docket number Q7450897, Mr. Cassius Magnus Hewson II please rise."

Now desperately looking around, the sheriff grabbed Cassius by the elbow ushering him up to the defendant's bench. His movements were awkward due to the cuffs on both his legs and his hands.

Reading silently over the charges, Judge Grissom looked down at Cassius dispassionately and asked directly, "Mr. Hewson when you surrendered to the Kannapolis Police Department you were mirandized correct?

"Yes, your honor."

"Wonderful. Do you have an attorney here to help represent you on the charges that are about to be read?

"Yes ma'am. My mother was supposed to hire an attorney to be present with me and speak the alleged charges."

Gazing around the room to ascertain who would be representing him Judge Grissom looked confused, "Where is your counsel?"
Now in full panic Cassius swiveled his head left and right hopelessly looking for anyone to help him defend himself.

"Ma'am they must be running,"

Before he could finish his sentence, "If you cannot afford an attorney one will be appointed you. Bill? Who do we have on tap this evening that could be assigned?"

The clerk quickly searched through his list posted on desk and handed Judge Grissom the name in question.

Looking to her left where the public defenders who were on-call were seated, "Ms. Young? Looks like today is your lucky day."

A sharply dressed woman made her way from the side bench to stand directly beside Cassius nodding her head in greeting. His hands were shackled so a handshake was not possible.

"Your honor? A moment to confer with my client."

"Be my guest," Judge Grissom said already shuffling through the other cases that would need to be adjudicated today.

The list of charges seemed to go on forever sounding progressively worse as the list went on. Once the bailiff read off the charges,

Cassius could feel the eyes of everyone in the room on his back as he responded with a plea of not guilty to the charges. The judge reviewed the file again and determined that his bond would be set at one million dollars. Since Cassius didn't have access to any of his cash, he would remain in custody until the bond could be met. His court ordered attorney, Ms. Young, confirmed that she would be in touch with his parents immediately. Once done, she would request another bond hearing with money in hand so that he could at least rest at home until the trial.

Disappointed but still determined, Cassius followed the Sheriff down to booking. He would rather be here than hunted down by the LeBlanc's. Emptying his pockets and dumping the contents. Cassius waited while the Sheriff recorded his belongings and placed them in a manila envelope for safe keeping. Cassius signed the manifest which confirmed that what was recorded was true. He was handed a t-shirt, a jumpsuit, a pair of flip-flops, and was told to remain undressed so that any gang-related tattoos could be captured.

Before Cassius had left the company of the LeBlancs, he was escorted to a tattoo parlor and dropped off with a guard. The guard showed the tattoo artist a picture and indicated where they should go on his body. Cassius didn't care as long as they didn't put a bullet in his head like they did to those other guys at his house. He believed as long as he was alive, he was ahead of the game.

"Hewson, Cassius," The guard called making sure that the correct inmate corresponded with his list.

"Yes," Cassius answered trying to get this over as quickly as possible.

"I need you to remove all of your clothing and turn around please." Cassius did as instructed, blinking when the camera flashed even though he was facing the wall.

The officer sounded surprised when he said, "I would have never figured you for fresh meat." Shaking his head, the officer gave him the best advice he could, "Stay woke."

Cassius was confused and just figured that fresh meat meant that he was new to the prison system. All he wanted to do was get assigned to his jail cell where he figured it would be safe.

Clarity came later that night after lights- out. For some reason, Cassius thought that he had lucked out and he was in a cell by himself. He laid in the bottom cot looking up at the ceiling trying to figure out how he could beat the charges hanging over his head.

He just needed a good attorney. So preoccupied with his thoughts, he never heard the lock sliding on the door. Four men entered the cell crowding the already small space. They didn't say anything just jacked him up from the bunk, pressed him against the wall and pulled his pants and underwear down.

They saw what he couldn't see, six inches above the crack of his ass was a tattoo of a mermaid. On either side of his cheeks were tattoos of eyes. The translation was that he had been effectively marked as anybody's meat and a pedophile. The men surrounding him congratulated each other on their latest find.

Cassius tried to struggle. He tried to run but he was outnumbered. He screamed once and was punched so hard in the head that he blacked out. During the time that he was down, they stripped and placed a sock his mouth tying it with another sock almost muffling his pitiful pleas. The guard's words came back to him, "Stay woke." If he survived this night, he would never sleep again.

CHAPTER 7

The Great Escape

Detectives James Edwards and Andrew Rohan

Detectives Ed and Rohan sat at their desk eating a celebratory piece of bread pudding from Epic Chophouse. They'd actually had dinner there as well, but because it was a forty-five-minute drive, they had to take their desserts with them.

The case was picking up speed. All because of a high electricity and water bill. If the homeowners had not come back to the house to check on things, they would still be investigating murders across two counties. Well, that and a 911 call.

A 911 call came in from an anonymous caller who said that shots had been fired in a house off Brantley Road in Kannapolis. In the house was an injured Jamison and two men dead in Jamison's family room with single shots to the head from the gun found in Jamison Hewson's possession. That along with anonymous photos sent with Jamison and the man that was shot and killed at the Andino property, tying him to an attempted murder.

Between the house in Huntersville and the rental, Jamison Hewson would not be seeing daylight for a very long time.

Initially, when the police arrived at the house, they found a knocked-out Jamison Hewson in the bathroom, a nine-millimeter Ruger clutched tightly in his hand lying on his stomach. Once the gun was secured and removed, he was turned over on his back to see if he had any visible injuries. Once the pain registered in his mind, he woke up screaming, "They burned my ass! They burned my ass!"

When the medics tried to calm him, he couldn't sit still because of the pain. He screamed and passed out again. Blood had seeped from his pants onto the floor where they tried to sit him. Seeing the blood, they immediately turned Jamison over to see his pants soaked in blood. He had to be taken to the hospital so that the burn wounds could be treated. Jamison had been branded on not one but both butt cheeks with the "all seeing eye" of the Egyptians on the right and a mermaid on the left. Why they branded him in the ass was anyone's guess Ed thought until Rohan saw the pictures taken by the Forensic Team and explained what those symbols would mean to those on the inside.

"They are going to wear his ass out – literally," Rohan chuckled and walked around to his side of the desk.

Curious as to Rohan's cryptic comments, Ed stared at his longtime partner. Knowing exactly what he was searching for, Rohan pulled out a book he kept in his desk drawer that detailed what different tattoos represented in the criminal world. Rohan pointed to a picture and Ed read silently then placing his hand over his mouth exclaimed a muffled, "Damn!"

The all-seeing eye meant different things in different cultures, but this poor schmuck, Ed thought silently. For the Russian's this type of tattoo on the front of the body right beneath the Adonis belt represented homosexuality, but this boy had them branded on his ass. There was no removal.

Flipping the page over, Ed saw the inscription for the Egyptian representation. It meant wrath. Combined with the mermaid literally translated that he has incurred wrath because he molested children.

Ed tried to muster some compassion but, in this case, Jamison Hewson earned it.

Standing down the hall from the nurse's station, Karen watched the ebb and flow of traffic. Considered a secure floor, only authorized people were allowed. Usually, the folks that were guest here weren't here by choice, but rather at the state's behest. The job paid a little extra, and protocol dictated she was never in the room alone with any patient, due to the risk of injury. Though the job was slightly dangerous, it did pay well plus the stories she collected about the folks that circulated through the doors kept her and her grandmother entertained for hours on end.

Karen was a Nursing Assistant by title but only a few weeks from graduating with her Licensed Practical Nurse. She worked the hospitals on the weekend because most of her week was committed to studies. Student loans were whopping her ass, but if she could just finish up these last weeks, Karen would finally reach the first stage of her goals. There were so many times she wanted to quit, but a friend she had met through class kept encouraging her to hang in there, and so she did.

Smart as hell to the point of almost being intuitive, Elaine Altman had to be sent from heaven. She was studying for her doctorate in nursing, which is how they met, ships crossing in the break room.

Seeing a friendly face, she saw the perfect opportunity to get the tea. Elaine was double-checking the lock on the med cart, when she acknowledged Karen's approach, "Hey girl hey!"

That was one of the weird things about Elaine, you could never catch her off guard. Karen was watching her while she approached, but somehow, Elaine knew someone was behind her and who that someone was.

Watching her stand to her full height of 5'10, Karen chuckled asking, "How do you do that?"

Looking perplexed, Elaine answered, "Do what?"
Karen could tell she honestly had no idea what she was referring to, so she just left it alone and jumped right to the heart of what she wanted, "Who's the new patient?"

"Room number?" Elaine had already moved back to her PC recording the time of the med cart check and docking the meter in its cradle so that it could sync up with the latest prescriptions and dosages. Every ounce of medication was recorded and monitored, especially the opioids. That was the thing about Elaine; she was always a body in motion.

"375A," Karen responded with curiosity.

"That would be Nunya – as in None of your business," she ended with straight out laughter.

"Ah girl come on! Give!" Karen pleased with her bottom lip in full pout position.

"Negative Grasshopper. In the words of Gandalf, the Wizard – YOU SHALL NOT PASS!" the word pass was accented with a gavel like motion pounding on the desk and a full hearty snicker. Karen rolled her eye in mock frustration and tried to hold in her laughter. Elaine was such a geek at times.

"You know the rules. You only need to be aware of the patients under your care. It's for your safety."

"I know I know," Karen capitulated.

Both Karen and Elaine paused as another set of officers came down the hall and stood in front of the patient's door. Karen watched the officers converse, all of them frowning. Whoever this person was, they must have done something horrible or pissed off the wrong people. Little did Karen know it was both, and things were about to get interesting.

North East Medical Center

Jamison Hewson

Jay tried to move his arm to shut the alarm off, but he felt like he was fighting through quicksand. Pain. Mind-numbing pain. Jay had never in his life felt this much pain. He tried to rise, but the room swam and down again he went. Struggling to focus, Jay struggled to understand just what was happening. Eyes dilating once dilated were coming back into focus and Jamison was able to see around the room. The beeping noise was from the IV drip. The machine had run out of fluids and was alerting the nursing staff.

Still confused, Jay again tried to rise and heard a rattling noise. Following the sound, Jay realized why he couldn't move. He was shackled to the bed, face down. That's when it all came back to him – the blow to the head, the searing heat, but most of all, the pain.

Tensing up, he heard footsteps entering the room. Turning his head, he saw the male nurse checking the stats on the monitor and then addressing the IV pump. Clearing his throat, he tried to ask questions.

"Where am I?"

"Good Evening Mr. Hewson." The male nurse said warmly walking around to the front of the bed so that he wouldn't have to strain too much to see him.

"You are at North East Medical Center in Concord, North Carolina. It is 7:30PM and you arrived this past Thursday. Today is Saturday. You suffered a concussion and have been in and out of coconsciousness for the last forty-eight hours. If all goes well, you will be released within the next twenty-four hours?"

"Why in the hell am I locked to this bed and why in the fuck does my ass hurt?"

"Well sir," the nurse intoned serious sly while scratching his nose, "We were hoping that you could tell us what you remember."

Jay laid there, eyes closed and tried to recall what happened, but all his mind would render were flashes of light and then, pain. It just hurt too much.

Frustrated and deflated, he repeated the first part of his question,

"The handcuffs?"

"The questions on handcuffs would need to be answered by the officers sitting outside," The nurse replied with calm patience.

"You mean you can't tell me anything?" Jay screamed his question frustrated. Crickets. All that Jay heard was the nurse moving around the room making sure that all alarms were off, and the meds were refilled in the pump. He snapped off his gloves, using his left foot, stepped on the lever that would open the garbage can.

A uniformed cop along with two plainclothes officers came into view and called his name, more than likely hearing part of the conversation that took place with the nurse.

"Mr. Hewson? My name is Officer Tarvy and these are Detectives Edwards and Rohan."

"Why am I handcuffed to this bed?"

"Mr. Hewson I am going to read you your rights."

"Rights for what? Take these fucking cuffs off me!"

"Sir you have the right to remain silent. Anything that you say from this moment forward can be used against you in a court of law."

Everything else was drowned out. Jay's mind was racing. He had been caught and was about to lose everything.

The officer's voice came back into focus again, "You have the right to an attorney. If you cannot afford an attorney, one will be provided for you."

Sliding in behind the officers, were a pair of very costly men's dress shoes. Clearing his throat, the stranger stepped forward into view.

"That would be me," Veneers blinging with a smile not quite reaching his eyes.

"My client will not be taking any questions now as you can see, he is heavily medicated." Dipping into the tailored suit, he pulled out two business cards.

"Robert Smith at your service. Now if you would give me a moment with my client, it would be greatly appreciated."

With that said, neither Ed nor Rohan had a choice. Both men looked at each other and walked out of the room, frowns firmly in place.

Once the room was empty, Robert turned to his newly acquired client and held a finger up to his mouth giving the universal sign for silence. Tapping his finger against his ear, indicating that big brother was listening.

"Son, they are charging you with numerous things the greatest of those being murder."

Rising from his bed in a pseudo push up Jamison denied forcefully, "I didn't do any of those things!"

"Which is why I'm here. To clear your good name, so don't you say a word. I'm working on getting a hearing, so we can get you back home and safe until the trial starts."

Jamison wasn't a dummy. There was no way in the world he was going to be able to afford bail and greater still, who in the world sent this attorney. His parents didn't have that kind of money.

"For now, say nothing and talk to no one."
Dumbfounded at his entire situation, Jamison agreed without argument.

Ed and Rohan

There celebratory lunch was cut short when they got the call from North East stating that Jamison Hewson was coming out of his coma. Whoever hit him rung his bell pretty good, causing a concussion. They just need five minutes to confirm what they already knew, but now none of that would happen.

"What we have on him is circumstantial for the sex trafficking, but there is no way that he's going to skate on those bodies found in the house he was renting.

"True, but don't you feel it? If this clown gets out on bail, he's gonna run."

"Shit! Murmured an agitated Rohan."

"Shit is right my friend. We need to ride him like a rented mule. I know a rabbit when I see one!"

Taking out the card that the attorney provided, Ed looked up at his partner. "There's still other work that can be done. Exactly how did our ass tatted friend get an attorney that quick?"

"Astute observation my friend! How did he get an attorney that fast, especially since he's been knocked out for a day or so?"

Looking grim, the partners headed out the door. It was time to follow the money.

CHAPTER 8

Sharper than a Laser

Ezra Nonnac

Ezra Nonnac stooped to the ground and picked up a hand full of dirt. Sifting it through his fingers, Ezra stood to his full seven-foot height, letting the clumps and small granules sift through his fingers and drift to the ground. He had selected this small plot of land to plant his garden. The land would need to be tilled during the fall then tilled again after the last frost.

Now his granddaughter by marriage, Savanah kept aloe plants around the perimeter of the shop. It was necessary because of the nature of her work. Since her brother Charleston was spending more time in Kannapolis, they had extended the space to include tools he could use for this newest hobby, making antique weapons. Since he had decided to remain in the Kannapolis for the winter, Ezra wanted to at least try to make it work. The first step was making this new land his own. Besides, it was time he passed on what healing knowledge he had on to his grandson as it was passed to him from his grandfather.

The giggling gave them away… always the giggling. Looking around to make sure that their mother was not in sight, Ezra made his way over to his great grandsons.

Daniel and David were the exact replica of he and his brother Nehemiah in temperament. Those boys had no fear and shied away from nothing. It drove their mother crazy but made Ezra long for the brother he lost many years ago.

They were surrounded by the pack so Ezra wasn't worried about their safety but if Savannah, their mother was to see them literally using his hunting dogs as pack horses, she would have a fit.

"Ninos! Get down right now before your mother sees you and spanks all three of us!"

A synchronized, "Aww" could be heard over the barking and yipping that began as he approached his pack. Princess the matriarch of the pack jumped down off a giant boulder that she was resting on and walked forward. As one, the boys ran for her, and with gentleness that was not typical of children so young, held out their hands in greeting and waited while Princess sniffed them gingerly. Then she did something totally uncharacteristic for such a wild and beautiful creature. Gently touching her nose to each of theirs then rubbing her rather large head up the side of their necks and their faces, almost in a doggy hug. She was marking them as one of her pack.

Ezra's heart swelled with pride. Princess accepted very few outside of her pack. That she would accept his blood as that of her own was extremely special and slightly scary.

"Daniel? David?" Christopher's deep voice could be heard inquiring across the yard.

Looking solemn but giving Princess a hearty hug, the boys took off running in the direction that they heard their father's voice, waving at their great-grandfather as they zoomed by. Ezra chuckled trying hard to remember when he had that much energy. While watching his boys with a smile as if the wind was lifting their feet, Princess made her way over leaning into his leg. Because of the sheer volume of her body mass, she rocked Ezra's legs, causing his body to sway back with force of her push.

"My Lady," he posed, looking down at his longtime friend. "I think it's time for one more run in the hills before the winter sets in."

Confirming his suggestion, Princess lifted her head and barked once, causing the pack to come from all over the yard, a total of thirteen. Ezra looked at all the beautiful creatures surrounding him and intoned, "It's time to hunt!"

Del heard Christopher's voice calling across the yard, looking for his sons. She had to laugh a little cause there was no telling what those wee terrors had gotten into, plus it gave her a slight break from facing reality. She had a flight to catch in a few days so that she could meet up with Z. They were headed to Bermuda for a quick getaway. Chastising herself mentally, it wasn't as if Z didn't know her, hell he knew her in the biblical sense. There was not a part of her body that he didn't know.

The flight length was supposed to be around four hours which would put her in a plane with the man that she has been avoiding with no way out, at least not unless she wanted to parachute into the Atlantic Ocean. That was the thing, she was tired of running. Del loved Z. She was woman enough to admit that to herself, but this step? In her gut, Del knew that this meeting would answer a definitive mark on their relationship, but would he accept all of her, even the things he didn't know? If she was going to commit, Z deserved to know everything. She would not go into her next relationships with secrets or lies. There was promise with this thing that she and Z had and she wanted to make it work.

There was something else niggling her. Ever since that day that Ezra caught that dumbass on the property with that young kidnapped girl, Del felt the need to patrol. Since she knew the wolves were on the property, she felt safe, but there were days she wanted to rove the woods with them, making sure the family was protected, or better still, make sure that no other little girl suffered the same fate that beautiful young girl suffered. Had those wolves not been patrolling the property there was no telling what would have happen to the poor baby before that animal snuffed out her beautiful light.

Restless, Del stopped packing and made her way out to the deck. A gentle breeze blew chimes attached to the porch causing a melodic tune to shimmer in the air. Her phone vibrated in her pocket, but she didn't bother looking. He was relentless when he wanted something and Del knew that Z was making sure that she was on schedule. Shaking her head, Del turned to look at the long winding road that led to the Andino's house.

Del saw his dogs before she saw him. They were running full out towards her full doggy grins intact and Del couldn't help but laugh. Bran and Brawny slowed to a light trot, still beelining for Del so she sat on the steps and waited for them to greet her. Charleston was not far behind jogging at a quick pace.

"Hey Babies!" Del exclaimed in a high pitch voice.
Wet noses pressed into Del's body, both ginormous dogs seeking a rub and attention. Charleston finally made it up the path, hands on his knees breathing heavy.

Del looked at her old Marine buddy shaking her head, "You've gotten soft! Thought you were sparing with Idris?"

Charleston's answer was a strong middle finger. Del hollered! Breathing heavily and trying to talk over her laughter, "You haven't lived until you see a few sets of eyes watching you from the woods. That shit is creepy as hell! And these two idiots took off running when they saw your house through the clearing, so I didn't have a choice but to take off after them.

Del couldn't stop laughing, "I thought you were a dog whisperer?" His body went ramrod straight and the man that had studied both anthropology and medicine spoke with authority, "Those are not dogs! Those are dire wolves. They shouldn't be here… hell alive for that matter!" Charleston ended his tirade on a "Shit!"

Del stopped laughing and looked at her friend. To Del, he was like a brother. A huge, handsome brother, but a brother, nevertheless. They had never been attracted to each over, but for as long as Del had known him, she felt this unmitigated urge to protect him. It was something that she couldn't explain yet something that Charleston understood. In fact, it was her urge to protect that made Del so good at recon and information. When they served together, Charleston would often remind her that her gift had saved countless lives. For Del it was embedded in her DNA, she had to find the answer.

Taking in her brother from another mother, Del realized something. He looked... different? He's picked up muscle. A lot of muscle! He had a backpack on this back, which for her wasn't unusual, but for Charleston it was peculiar.

"What's in the bag?"

Something for you actually. It came to the main house, certified mail. Savannah signed for it and put it on top of the fridge so that the boys couldn't get to it, but then she forgot about it. Charleston and Del looked at each other and laughed.

"Whatever it is it has some weight." Charleston took the bag off his shoulder, gently laying it down so that he could unzip it without dropping the contents.

The box was addressed from a solicitor's office in not far from the town she grew up in. But why would an attorney be sending her anything? Climbing the stairs that led to the house, Del distractedly held the door open while her welcomed company piled in and made themselves comfortable.

Sitting in the corner of his cell Cassius wanted to die, but more importantly he wanted Asa to die. All of this was her fault. It was because of her that he was sitting in this jail cell bleeding from places that made him cry every time he moved.

They labeled him a pedophile and the henna tattoos he had put it out there for all that went to the shower to see. He didn't rape or touch any children. It's what he screamed over and over when they were attacking him. Sometimes they just beat him. Anything was better than being raped, so he fought back hoping that they would knock him the fuck out so he wouldn't have suffered the indignity. His mother was missing in action and all he had was the court appointed attorney. Unless a miracle happened, he was stuck in this hell hole. None of it mattered anyway. Soon as lights were out, he was going to kill himself.

"Hewson!"

Cassius made his way to the front of the cell, placing his hands through the small square. He had to keep appearance normal even though he was slowly dying inside.

"Mail Call,"

Cassius waited patiently for the guard to pass on the letters that were in his hands. The guard looked at him with pity and said with a straight face, "Shame. Stay woke man!"

There was nothing he could say or do, but just take the mail that was in his extended hand. There was a letter from a Christian group praying for his soul salvation and one from the court. He didn't need wishful thinking he needed to get out of this hell hole, so he ripped open the letter from the court.

Skimming through the note Cassius found his first ray of hope. His court date had been moved up to tomorrow. Something must have happened. Maybe his mother came through. Closing his eyes in a brief moment and breathed a sigh of relief. This had to be a good sign.

CHAPTER 9

"The White Rose"

Rhoda sat in her office watching the sun set over Lake Norman. The house was on a peninsula that jutted out into the lake, surrounded on three sides by water. Though the water was not as blue as the ocean she loved, it reminded her of home.

Her work here was almost done. Her grandsons were progressing along nicely with their new responsibilities, but in no way was Rhoda fooled. Zalmon had too much of his father in him to take being marginalized lightly. Even now she knew that both he and his imbecile son were plotting on how to regain what they lost, but as usual they could see the forest for the trees.

Rhoda had hopes that her boys would at minimum tolerate each other but that went to hell in a handbasket years ago. Legally there was only so much she could do with the corporation, but there were other ways that she could make sure that Zebulon, Fernando, and Kedar and any of their descendants would want for anything.

“Yarena?” Rhoda said distractedly eyes focused on documents on her monitor.

Pencil and pad in hand, Yarena moved quickly in the room, prepared to take notes on whatever the boss lady needed.

Yarena Eriksson was the baby sister of Eric and Peter. She was every bit as lethal as her brothers but didn’t want to spend the rest of her life protecting anyone. She, like Rhoda had an affinity for numbers plus the things she could do computers was almost on par with her grandson Fernando.

It’s time to put operation Gold Rush into play. I want the paperwork no later than Friday for review and once notarized, secured.
“Yes ma’am. Is there anything else you need?”

“A nice vacation?” Rhoda chuckled. No dear, for now that will be all. Rhoda took her glasses off, spun her chair around and gazed out the window once again. The sun was going down and in a sense it was symbolic. She had loved and she had lived. By no means perfect because so many stupid mistakes were made along the way. But what she would never do, is concede defeat. She would fight till her last breath. It was in her DNA and there was no other way she knew how to live her life. While she didn't win every battle, she sure as hell left her mark.

"Ma'am?" Yarena spoke softly trying to grab Rhoda's attention. Rhoda turned back around, slight smile on her face in question. Your son has sent over some additional documents that he says are urgent for your review.

Rhoda sighed in disgust. A hard head makes soft bottom. Please inform my son that the item, Rhoda held out her had to see the copy that Yarena held, viewing them quickly to confirm the region that it should have been sent to, "that Kedar, as per protocol will handle any questions or concerns about our South Pacific hubs and that for this consultation an additional seven thousand five hundred dollars will be billed.

Yes ma'am. Also, your husband would like a word as soon as you have a free moment.

Translation, he cursed poor Yarena up one block and down the next. Thank you Yarena. We're done for the evening. You can call it a night.

Yarena wore multiple hats in the BCI organization. Her primary role was to be Rhoda's personal assistant. As they traveled all over the world, Rhoda made sure that Yarena had rooms wherever she stayed so calling it a night was just as simple as going to the opposite end of the house to the guest quarters.

"I've confirmed line one is clear and ready when you are." Giving Rhoda a sympathetic look as she closed the door, Rhoda laughed out loud. She had been waiting on this conversation for the last day or so and was surprised that Zalmon Sr. showed this much restraint. The line was secure so she could speak freely. She had security sweeps on all lines both here and abroad on a regular basis. Placing the phone on her desk to speaker, Rhoda made a call that traveled across the Atlantic to reach a distance receiver.

"You will remove those bastards as Executives and reinstate my son and grandson immediately!" The scratchy voice screamed on the other end.

"Well hello darling! I've missed you too," Rhoda intoned sweetly.

"Cut the bullshit and I mean it Rhoda! What do you think you are doing? Have you lost your mind? Apparently, you have! Zalmon if you let one more curse word rolls off your tongue while speaking to me there will be a misunderstanding. You have forgotten what I am and who I am. I am your wife and the mother of your children and you will address me with the courtesy that title deserves!"

The line went quiet for a few beats while Zalmon gathered himself. He knew the limits of his boundaries with Rhoda and right now he was tipping around the edge. He had found that the trick was seeing just how far he could push. Zalmon knew that there was no love lost between the two at this point, only duty. While he would always cherish her for the gift that she gave him, his son, the days of romanticism were well past.

"It appears my dear that we are at an impasse. Black Cesar International is my corporation. I will not have anyone but my bloodline sitting in seats of power. Period!"

Rhoda began to laugh. Hard. All these years and this pompous fool thought that he could rewrite history. Too old to argue, Rhoda tried another approach.

"So, you condone the acts of your son and grandson? That they were running a house of ill repute and financing it with underage girls?"

Zalmon senior began to sputter in protest, so Rhoda pressed on,

"Or the fact that while in their tender care, two of those girls died?"

Though they technically were not physically in the possession of

Invictus when one of them was strangled in a field, the result was still the same. She was abducted because of her grandson and his greed. That little girl had done time trapped in a house, though beautiful, doing things that were against her will.

"He's young Rhoda. He made a mistake."

"Mistake you say? A mistake is forgetting your wallet at home, or leaving the light on in kitchen, not running underage girls and boys in and out of a house for the pleasure of depraved old men!"

Her comments were met with silence, because there was morally no excuse for what Invictus did. Furthermore, there was no way in the world he didn't know. Her son and grandson got their arrogance honestly. Zalmon always believed that he was the sun rose and sat on his intelligence. His prodigy believed the same. It was fun to let them believe as such. What Zalmon didn't want is for her to become irritated. Enough was enough and the time for civility was almost at an end.

"Well," Zalmon said on a sigh. Which meant that he was beginning to concede to her argument.

"While we were able to recoup some of the losses finically, word has gotten around, and we have lost some contracts. No one wants to deal with anyone trading children."

"What?"

"Turn your hearing aid up Dear. We lost roughly ten percent of our US contracts. The sales of some of the properties obtained, only covered a fraction of a percent of our expenses on the east coast for a month. So, tell me, who should be held responsible for this debacle?"

Hearing the financial impacts of his grandson and son's mistake brought everything into focus. Clearing his throat, Zalmon senior, took his righteous tone down, "Well, I understand that you're doing what needs to be done to teach them a lesson, but to be clear this is only temporary."

Rhoda, heard what was stated, but as usual, she ignored her husband when he was making unreasonable demands.

"Enjoy your evening!"

"You the same!"

Rhoda disconnected the call sitting back in her chair again. Her mind was spinning. For sure the table was set. There was no way that her husband would allow what he believed to be the rightful heirs to his empire not have complete control. She knew he was plotting something, but the question was, exactly how far would he go.

CHAPTER 10

Unraveling the Mystery

Charleston sauntered into the house, making himself at home while the dogs went to their favorite place beside the recliner that sat across from the fireplace. Shifting the backpack off his shoulder, Charleston walked over the recliner and placed the box in Del's lap.

Del looked at the box apprehensively but Charleston wasn't having it.

"Girl that box has been sitting on my sister's fridge for a month. Either you open it, or I will."

Giving herself a mental shake, Del began to dismantle the box, now curious about what was inside. She wasn't disappointed. There was a small beautifully stained mahogany box carved with intricate symbols along with an envelope addressed to her.

There was no return address, so Del just ripped it open. Script was neat and reminded her of old handwritten love letter. No one wrote like this anymore. Carefully unfolding the note, Del began to read.

Dearest Sister,

It has taken some time to find you, but I never gave up. I know that this letter will place you into various states of disarray, but there is no way that I could ease this burden or blessing… depending on your view.

The box enclosed contains your inheritance from our mother who loved you more than life itself. I hope that you will wear them with pride and cherish them as we all did you.
So that you are at least assured that this is not a hoax, I have enclosed a copy of a small painting that was made of all of us, along with your birth certificate. Please know that you are loved and there was not a moment in time that we were not searching for you. When you are ready, we would like to meet with you in person. I have enclosed my business card. Day or night, when you are ready don't hesitate to call.

Love Always,
Zaire

There were no words. Del looked down at the paper again, one tear trailing its way down her cheek. She never cried, but this? This was more than she could bare. She had a brother – one that had been looking for her for years. Gently Del picked up the arm bangles admiring the intricate designs. They were stunning!

She had always wondered what her birth family was like. Did her mother love her? What happened to her birth father? Did she have any brothers or sisters? All those thoughts tumbled through her mind as she looked at her beautiful inheritance. It suddenly became too much to process. She couldn't breathe! She had to get out of the house! Standing abruptly, Del clutched the beautiful bangles in her hands for a moment then handed them and the box to one of the two living beings she trusted the most. Their eyes met and Charleston gave a quick nod. He had no idea how she was feeling as he was blessed to have a happy and healthy relationship with his parents. What he did understand was grief, the grief of not knowing and for that he gave his sister in spirit – space.

Del exited the house and went into the backyard, pacing in circles around the fire pit. Walking helped her think. She needed to at least try to put the pieces of the puzzle together. She circled the pit two, three, four times, each time her heart rate picking up until she was teetering on panic then the dam broke. Throwing her head back she let out a primal scream and dropped to her knees first then to the flat of her bottom and wept uncontrollably.

Hearing her wale, Charleston placed the box on the couch and rushed outside. Before he could approach, they came swiftly from the woods, circling her, closing ranks just like they did in the field if a soldier was down. The alpha male trusted that the rest of the pack would monitor the threat while he assessed the wounded. Trotting up to Del, he nudged her face with his nose licking gently trying to get her attention. His ministrations were a success as Del reached her arms around him and held him close.

At this point Charleston began to panic. Those were wolves, dire wolves at that and not some domesticated pet. By virtue of his employment, Charleston had seen dogs of all sizes and breeds. Big dogs didn't bother him, hell he owned two. The fact that the dog could sit on its hind quarters and still be taller than Del was unique but not unusual. The problem was that chest was about two and a half feet wide along with eye teeth that were barely concealed by his top lip.

Del's scream was like a country alarm causing anyone that was outside and near press their way towards the woeful sound. Christopher and Ezra pulled up in Christopher's old Chevrolet truck. Charleston could never remember the year of the truck but what he did know is that it was a beauty to behold. Candy apple red with a chrome grill. Christopher had a V10 in that baby and when she cranked, she rumbled with authority.

Charleston watched the men approach from the side of the house but even before they came into view, a sharp growl cracked the air. Feeling a little insulted that wolves didn't give him the same reception when he came from the house. Charleston waited with a slight smirk on his face to see what Ezra would do.

To Charleston's surprise, it wasn't Ezra who stepped up to defuse the situation, it was Christopher. He spoke a command rapidly in a language that was, if Charleston was not mistaken, Middle Eastern and more specifically not common. It felt… ancient. The words were accompanied by a shrill whistle.

Both he and Del were fluent in several languages because it was detrimental in their former life. And while they never expected to have any use for it state side, this was all very disconcerting. Either the words or the whistle snapped Del from her grief. Still holding on to the giant wolf's neck with tears still streaming slowly in her sitting position on the ground, she looked up at the small but growing crowd watching her fall apart. Eyes now half cast, "You know Ezra, eventually you and Honey will help me understand how both of you speak Coptic, a language that belonged to people long since departed from this earth.

No one saw her approach but the wolves and once they recognized her presence, they swarmed her in masse yipping for attention. Honey's broad smile seemed to lift the tangible gloom that had descended on the small group gathered. "There are some things little one that you are still not ready to know."

Reaching out her hand, the matriarch of the pack pressed her way through her children and rubbed her head against Honey's outstretched hand. Stooping down, Honey embraced her friend. The alpha female rubbed her head against the side of Honey's face in greeting causing Charleston once again to slightly freak out inside. There were words whispered between the two that no one heard, but once they broke from their embrace and Honey stood, the alpha female tilted her head to the sky and let out a howl that was both haunting and beautiful at the same time. Even Bran and

Brawnie who clearly understood self-preservation and stayed in the house during the entire event, joined their voices in with the rest of the pack singing to the sky in only a language that they could understand.

Christopher, Ezra and Del smiled while Charleston continued to stare in disbelief. "Is anyone going to recognize the fact that we literally have a pack of long extinct prehistoric wolves wandering around the property?"

Ignoring Charleston's question, Honey walked over to Del unbothered, reaching out her hand to assist her off the ground.

Once she was standing, Honey enfolded Del in a soul quenching hug that quite frankly made Del slightly uncomfortable.
"Now Little One, let's go in the house and you can tell us what has you crying out to the universe in despair."

CHAPTER 11

Free Bird

"All rise!" The bailiff's strong voice reverberated around the room cause those that heard to push from the benches and chairs lining the court room.

"Court is now officially in session. The Honorable Senora C. Williams will be presiding."

An older black woman moved swiftly up the stairs to her chair, cracking open her laptop to review any new notes while the bailiff continued on with the opening announcements.

"Please make sure that all cell phones are turned off. There will be no talking while court is in session. If you need to speak with your attorney, a small window of opportunity will be given before your case is heard, or feel free to step outside the courtroom.

Defendants, please be advised that if you do not respond when your name is called you could be sited as absent and a bench warrant will be issued for your arrest. We have surprisingly full docket, so it is critical that when you hear your case called that you move with purpose. Attorney's whose clients are being transported to the court room by the Sherriff's office can step outside now and have a word with them in the Tank."

With the last parting statement, the bailiff turned to the Clerk of Court to verify if everyone was ready to begin.

Jamison Hewson sat on that hard as wooden bench gingerly, his torso shifting his bottom from cheek to cheek desperately trying to find a comfortable position. His wounds were healing, but the entire affair was a pain in the ass… literally. He had no idea still who mystery person that was sponsoring his defense, but neither did he care. He just needed to get through the day. According to his attorney, he needed to keep his mouth shut. So that's what he planned to do.

Robert Smith did not disappoint. Sharper than the board of health, he sauntered into the tank, searching over the sea of chained prisoners chained to the benches in a way that allowed them little to no movement. For security purposes, prisoners were housed in a separate room parallel to the court room. Once it was time for their case to be heard, they were brought into the courtroom, but only to a small plexiglass box large enough to fit the chained defendant and an officer. A safety measure put into place after a defendant was killed by a family member that didn't want to wait on justice.

"Alright Bud, I need you to hang in there for just a few more hours and you should be out," he intoned with confidence.

"What makes you so sure that I'm gonna walk," Jamison asked suspiciously.

“The two degrees that sit on my wall at the corner of Trade and Tryon Street. I said out and not walk. We have a lot of work to do before this comes to trial, if we can’t get the charges dropped. Now your freedom will not come without restrictions, but I’m positive that those provisions would be way more tolerable than your current one.”

The last was said with a serious tone that made Jamison look at his attorney a little differently. Nodding his head curtly, there was nothing he could do but wait and see how everything unfolded. Nothing else was said as Mr. Smith walked toward the guarded door and flashed his badge so that he could exit.

Cassius sat on the Transport van waiting to be moved from the van then into the courthouse. The wait wasn’t long as he shuffled in the almost too small plastic slides he was issued. He paused just a moment to look up at the sky and breath the fresh air, to see a crow caw in a nearby tree. While to the average person it was mundane, but when you’ve you had your freedom snatched away it becomes an entire new ball game.

He was moved through a series of tunnels and finally to a small room where inmates were housed. It must have been a slow day as there were few prisoners waiting for their time to appear before the judge. He was surprised at who he saw next.

Looking up at her, he nodded slightly confused, “Attorney Young?”

“Mr. Hewson, I apologize that we couldn’t get a hearing sooner, but the docket was filled. Based on what the prosecution has presented thus far, I believe I can get you out on bail under the Electronic Monitoring Program. You’d need to reside with your parents, and you would be house bound until the trial.”

Cassius was trying to process what she was saying but that all depended on if his parents would be willing to let him stay at their home until the trial. Considering the fact that he had not heard from his mother in the months that he had been locked up, that small beacon of light was squashed. At this point, none of it really mattered. There was a sheet and a couple of bars waiting on him when he got back to his cell. For now, he'd just go along with the flow. It would all be over soon.

Doing something he hadn't done in a long time, show humility. Looking up as his attorney solemnly, "Thank you for everything that you've done. I really appreciate it."

Smiling sharply, "Don't thank me just yet. All this is contingent we get for the judge this morning. Fingers crossed we'll have you at your mother's house by lunch."

Cassius just nodded his head, convinced that this was all a waste of time, but not letting his true emotion show. All this over a fat bitch who couldn't just take that fact that he no longer wanted her. If Asa had just gave him the ring back and went on about her business none of this would have happened. He could be right now on a beach, soaking up sun with the woman that he really loved. Nora stilled loved him. She just didn't want to see him like this. It was her love that sustained him in the hell that he had lived in for the past several weeks. Maybe if this actually panned out, he could hold her in his arms again. Thoughts moving from dark to light, Cassius waited patiently for the proceedings to begin. His fate hung in the balance.

CHAPTER 12

Release the Kraken

It was times like these that Del wished she had the skills of Savannah with all these people now gathered in her living room. The home training, she received from her mother kicked in and she remembered her manners.

"Would anyone like anything to drink," she asked, hands now twisting in nervousness. Realizing her nervous tick was on display for the world to see, Del forced her hands to her sides. Several

"No's" Del didn't know what to do next. Bran and Brawnie sensing her distress, both walked over to her pushing against her legs. Using that as a que to go sit down, Del made her way over to her favorite chair and unceremoniously plopped, sliding the chair back with the force of her movement.

Not one to wait on ceremony Honey was direct, "So what happened?" Before going outside, Charleston had placed the box on the table beside her chair, so Del grabbed it and handed it to Honey.

"Not sure if you and Ezra knew, but I was adopted. I never knew my birth mother or father. My adoptive parents never hid the fact that I was not theirs but neither did they love me any less. They kept what little information they received from the adoption agency and held it until I was eighteen. To be honest, I didn't want to know who my birth parents were. My adoptive parents gave me all the love I needed and more. I never wanted for anything. I felt like, at the time that looking for the people who didn't want me was a betrayal."

Both Honey and Ezra looked at her with understanding. Their somber expressions gave her the courage to continue.
"It wasn't until they both passed away that I looked at the adoption papers. It was included in the legal papers that laid out the estate. Hell, I had the power of the federal government at my fingertips so instead of hunting down terrorist, I tried to track down the folks that gave me away."

Taking a deep breath, Del stood and walked over to the small table set that stood against the wall. Grabbing a glass, she poured herself some Tahitian Treat moonshine in a glass, Del took a healthy swing. Turning around she faced her audience again and continued.

"What did you find?" Christopher asked.
Inhaling deeply, "Not a damn thing. It was like they disappeared off the face of the earth." Del responded, heat rising in her voice. Ezra held out his hand, gingerly holding the letter from her brother while Christopher admired the bracelets.

"Charleston gave me that box today. I looked and couldn't find anything, yet this man claims to be my brother and says he has information on my family. The analyst in me finds it curious that this man was able to find me here, in North Carolina, in this small town. I mean while I visited here before, I just recently sat down roots. I have never really had a home due to the work that I did for the military. Well, outside of my parents, which I never listed for security reasons."

Del looked at Charleston when she made the last statement. There were some things that they never spoke about, their time in the military was one. There were reasons behind their secrecy, and it was for the benefit of everyone one she loved that some things remain left unsaid.

Del had that prickly feeling rising up the back of her neck and inherently knew that Honey had her full focus on her. She was not disappointed when she turned and faced an intently focused Honey.

Honey stared intently at Del then posed, "What does your heart tell you?"

Turning to face Honey Del lamented, "My heart somedays is still twelve, listening to my parents tell me that they were not my birth parents; wondering what was so wrong with me that my birth parents didn't want me."

Honey nodded with empathy, urging her to finish the thought.

"The thirty-something me feels like by looking for the one who gave me life is somehow betraying the ones that were my life. I was truly blessed with the parents that I had and still cry every day because I miss them so damn much."

Every person in the room had their own personal journey with grief. The pain never truly leaves you it lingers making itself known at the most inconvenient time.

"Well Little One, this is not our fight, but we will fight for you, or your happiness that is," Honey said with a smile.

"But what am I going to find now that I didn't find with the might of the United States military?"

"A crack? You know as well as I do that often time information is often released in small increments. Maybe enough time has passed that what you couldn't find before is ready to be found."

Holding up the business card Charleston continued, "Now you have a new starting place that looks to be a solid lead."

"And besides, you are family little girl! If anyone thinks that they can use something as sensitive as your birth parents to get your attention or cause you harm in anyway, well, they deserved to be hunted by the pack because that's what's exactly going to happen," Ezra ended on a bass rumbling grumble.

As if on que, the pack began to howl again causing Charleston to declare loudly, "So y'all just gonna sit here while a pack of millennia extinct wolves howl as if he summed them," tilting his head towards Ezra.

Honey threw her head back and laughed loudly and warmly while Christopher dropped his, but not before Charleston could see the smile on his face. Only Ezra had the grace to look innocent, that was until his two treacherous dogs leaned back their heads and joined in with the Kugs in their lamentation.

Looking at his two previously faithful hounds, Charleston shook his head and mumbled, "Ain't this about a…."

“All Rise! The Honorable Senora Williams presiding.” The bailiff intoned with respect. Everyone in the courtroom stood quietly while Judge Williams made her way to the dioceses. Adjusting her robe so that she could sit comfortably, Judge Williams tapped her laptop to make it active and began looking at the list of dockets that flashed into view.

The Bailiff read off the first docket number and court began. That cadence went on for the next two hours with each case being heard and a ruling being made until they called the docket number for Cassius. Cassius was led into a small holding box that allowed him to see the courtroom. His mind was already set on the fact that he was never going to leave his current hell. The prosecutor and the judge had a quick back and forth and then his attorney spoke up, attempting to justify why he would be a good candidate for the program.

It was all happening so fast that Cassius almost missed the prosecutor agreeing to his attorney’s terms. Shaking his head to make sure he was awake and hearing the conversation correctly, Cassius slumped unceremoniously to the chair causing the sheriff in charge of his security to pause the hearing to make sure that he didn’t need medical assistance. In his head all he could hear was house arrest, house arrest, house arrest bouncing around in his brain. She had done it. The attorney had gotten him out of the hell hole that Asa had put him in, and he was going to be free.

The rest of the events went by in a blur and seemed surreal. The terms of the house arrest were simple. Cassius would remain in his parent’s house until the trial and would only be allowed to visit his attorney. Outside of that, he was restricted to the perimeter of his parent’s yard. The terms were effective immediately. Apparently, his father felt it more prudent to have him under his thumb at home versus the stigma of having a son locked up in jail. His parents actually attended court and were ready to receive him once he went through processing, receiving his new piece of jewelry courtesy of the state of North Carolina.

Standing outside the courthouse in a brand-new Polo shirt and khakis that his mom had purchased, it all seemed like a bad dream, the last weeks that he had spent in jail. Things were beginning to look up. Looking at his attorney again with new light in his eyes, Cassius could not thank her enough for her persistence. Before he could say anything, she beat him to the punch, "It is imperative that for the duration of your house arrest that you follow every rule the judge stated. Do not try to contact any one and I do mean anyone that is even remotely associated with your case! Let me work to get to the bottom of what really happened. Once you get some rest over the next couple of days, your parents are going to bring you into the office for an in-depth conversation of the events that led you to be locked up. I need you to use this time to truly think about the events. No detail is unimportant and can me be the difference between a misdemeanor or life in prison. If your cousin Jamison tries to contact you, call my office immediately!
She had kept her promise so Cassius would try his best to keep his, starting with the truth. "Trust me Ms. Young, Jamison Hewson is the last person I plan to talk to. As soon as he attempts to contact me, you will be the first person to know."

CHAPTER 13

On Your Mark

Jamison stood outside the Cabarrus County Courthouse stunned. That son of a bitch had done it. He was a freeman, well out on bail, but a freeman, nevertheless. The Shark, and Jamison had begun to call him sauntered towards him briefcase in hand with that toothy grin in place, hand outstretched waiting on the handshake. Jamison took it gladly, happy to be out of that hellhole for the time being. Now it was time to find his punk ass cousin and make sure that he didn't say shit.

"Our car is waiting just around the corner," he mumbled placing his hand at the small of Jamison's back urging him towards the gray Range Rover idling close to the curve. Jerking his head ever so slightly up and to the right, Jamison shifted his eyes quickly taking in the camera that was recording his every move. Jamison slid in the car gingerly noting that a doughnut was left in the seat obviously for his use.

As the car took off smoothly heading towards Church Street, The Shark made his pitch. "There were too many cameras there for my liking strategically placed to pick up information. From now on, we speak either in my office or on this." Opening up a side panel in the car, he grabbed a box containing a cell phone.

"You have to know that they are watching you. The only reason that you were released is so you can lead them to the bigger fish. I suspect it was at the behest of the Feds, but I won't have that confirmation until later today."

Jamison looked at his attorney with confusion. He didn't have any contact. He and Sean worked those dumbass kids on their own, but he was not about to say anything.
"What do you know about Black Caesar International?"

"Not a thing."

"Try again," he said with a no-nonsense tone making Jamison look up from the new I-Phone 10.

"You applied for a position at the Port of Charleston. Why?"

"Because they pay good money," Jamison said with a shrug of his shoulders.

"Son you have a degree in accounting and would make way more money in their corporate office instead of the dock job you applied for, so again I ask what do you know about BCI."

Not at all scared of the change in topic, but more interested preserving his freedom, Jamison countered with a question of his own, "While appreciate your professionalism in handling my case, I insist on paying my on fees."

"That ship has sailed Mr. Hewson. It sailed when you verbally agreed for me to be your attorney, then signed the contract, which is binding by the way, that all legal expenses would be paid by Neith LLC. By your legal and notarized signature, our contract states that you will work for corporation for a term of one year for a small salary in lieu of legal services received.

Jamison didn't remember any of that. The only thing he did remember is that .... He showed up in the hospital room shortly after those cops did. He didn't remember signing anything, but ...

"You got me!" Jamison shouted, realizing too late what he had signed.

Sly smile on his lips, his attorney continued. "My employer and your new boss need to see you immediately. Let's not keep him waiting."

They had won this round, but at this point, Jamison wasn't too sure exactly who "they" were. What he did know, is that once he got his bearings straight, he would be hell on wheels, contract or no.

Fernando checked his watch for what felt like the two hundredth time. He was almost as nervous now as he was the first time that they had met. Cupping his hand to his mouth he did a breath check... and an Altoid was critical right now.

Del called and said she wanted to meet up before they took their mini vacation. In his mind, he was praying that she didn't get cold feet. He needed her to know that he was one hundred percent hers and there was nothing that would stop him from loving her. There was nowhere she could run because he would always find her. Tonight, he was downtown - well, not quite downtown about a mile north east of downtown. He was in the upcoming NoDa District. Once a thriving mill district, North Davidson back in the day use to be filled with proud African American homeowners until the collapse of manufacturing closed the mills. Major league sports and gentrification took care of the rest.

His grandfather along with some other investors had the foresight to invest in properties, a lot of properties, attempting to help those that had been were being disenfranchised. Over time they were able to purchase a large swath of the community very quietly. Once the time was ripe, they executed their long-term strategy for the area, affordable housing.

Looking out the window, he smiled, and an image of his mother came to mind. When they first broke ground on the construction of this building, Fernando had his mother in mind. While he needed to make a profit, he also wanted a place that single mothers could stay and have no fear of being evicted.

There were times in his past where his mother worried where their next meal would come from or where they would lay their head. If not for the kindness of the Andino Family, they would have been in a world of hurt. Plus, if he recalled correctly, Christopher taught him how to throw his first punch, ironically against his twin brother Christian. Fernando smiled at the memory. Those boys were always into to something and made his childhood bearable. There were some things that money would never buy and the kindness of the Andinos was something that could never be repaid. The key turning the lock in the door grabbed his attention and broke him from the journey down memory lane. Tossing his hair over his shoulder, he made his way to the front of the condo with a slight smile on his face. What could he say? She made him happy.

The Range Rover pulled smoothly into the valet parking to allow both he and his attorney out. Silently Jamison admired the stonework. Somebody had money, he thought to himself.

"Right this way Mr. Hewson," the crocodile said with a smile. That's what he reminded him of now. Always smiling, but that smile never quite reaching his eyes.

The entrance to the building raised his suspicion, but the interior nailed it on the head. Even though Jamison was not begging for bread, there was no way he could afford to pay the fee that he knew this law office charges their clients. The dye had been cast so at this point there was nothing left to do but see what colors would emerge.

A very tall woman that should have been on someone's magazine cover came out to greet them with a smile on her face. It was hard to tell her age, but she was stunningly beautiful. Her hair was in micro locs pulled back into a severe bun. The locs were hers and he could tell that by the way they were interlocked at the root. The bun was a pretty good size so that meant unbound, her hair at minimum had to come do to roughly mid back. Jamison was stunned and just couldn't stop staring. In the age of faux beauty, it was refreshing to see a woman that was natural. Her nails, though manicured, were not overlaid with acrylic. The suit she wore hung in all the right places not revealing everything but just enough to make you want more.

"Mr. Hewson? Mr. Hewson are you okay?" Jamison snapped out of the trance she had put him in to see a hand outstretched, waiting to be shook and he just standing there like a knot on a log.

Face reddening slightly, his mind caught up with his body and he extended his hand. Her grasp was firm and sure as she leaned in shaking his hand, he could smell the light floral fragrance that she wore. She made him think of lilies and fresh water.

"Thank you for coming in to see us today. I think the opportunity provided is one that is mutually beneficial to both parties. If you will follow me, we head to my office to discuss the final details of your contract."

Looking at down at the hand that was holding his in a firm handshake, Jamison, just couldn't shake the feeling of falling. His mind was in a fog and despite the explanation that the Crocodile had given, none of this made sense to him. Maybe if he saw the written contract and verified his signature, he would feel a little more at ease. Even then, he still trusted no one, let alone these crafty motherfuckers.

“Mr. Jamison?”

Raising his head up slowly to meet the beautiful woman’s eyes Jamison tried to take a step back, but she grasped his hand firmly. Jamison tried not to panic but it was too late. He knew the look of death and this lady? Jamison knew that if he dealt with these people his mother would be identifying his body on a cooling board.

“Is there something wrong?”

“Just tired. It’s been a very rough couple of days. Looking back the way he came there were two security guards standing at the door. There was no way back. They only way to go now was forward.

Jamison painted on the mask that he always wore, “After you ma’am”.

Del tried hard to focus, but Fernando, well in his defense, he was being the perfect gentlemen. The problem was the cologne. It was wafting in her direction subtly at first, like when he opened the door and leaned in for a kiss on the cheek. He must have had a diffuser because she could smell the relaxing fragrances beginning to put her mind at ease. Inhaling deeply, Del’s mind began to slow from one thousand miles a minute to a nice steady seventy. There was so much she needed to tell him.

Walking away Fernando looked over his shoulder while she seemed frozen in place. Time stopped and Del got a glimpse of the person underneath it all. He was Z, Zebulon Fernando White, but he was so much more. There were times in the past when they were together that Del thought, she knew everything about her lover. These past couple of months taught her all the things she thought she knew and more.

Pivoting on his heel he turned to face Del. Head cocked to the side with locs slipping out of his bun placed haphazardly on top of his head, his eyes searched her face.

In her mind, Del had planned out what she was going to say. She wanted to tell him about the letter and her newfound family, but there was something about the way he looked at her combined with the scents invading her body that she went from worry to want. She wanted Fernando like her next breath.

Lifting his chin slightly, he motioned her towards the spot where he was standing. No words were exchanged, but that wasn't unusual for their relationship. Standing face to face, they were close enough now that her foot rested between his instep.

"Once you touch me it's a wrap." Looking at him intently, Del weighed her options. She could either worry about what she couldn't change, or she could bask in sexual pleasure that wouldn't end until she begged him to stop and Del begged no one.

Taking both hands and using her index fingers, Del ran her fingers across his eyebrows, then lightly with one hand down the bridge of his nose. He was staring at her so intently, she wanted to break his concentration, even if for a moment. It didn't work. Gone was the sweet Fernando that he showed to the business world and in his place was Z, ruthless hacker and all around badass.

Picking her up at the waist, which still amazed Del because she was not a small girl, he walked her over to the island in the kitchen. There was no foreplay or romantic words, just the fulfilling of the promise made. Making simple work of her shoes and pants, Z laid her back on the island and treated her like a platter, he feasted.

Head back resting on the cool granite, Del could hear the chair sliding forward. She waited with anticipation of the first stroke, but it didn't come from that magnificent tool in his pants, it came from his wicked tongue. The same sweet way they greeted each other with a kiss, Z now did to the lips between her hips. Before she could even inhale, the orgasm flowed from her pussy to the back of her neck causing her back to arch and her arms to flail, hand reaching for anything to anchor her.

The feast continued as he slowly circled her clit causing her legs to shake. Never missing a stroke with his tongue, Z grabbed each thigh, placing them over his shoulder so that nothing would block him from his goal which was total access. Mind fragmenting with pleasure, Del tried to pull back, but that only made Z growl and clamp her thighs tighter.

This is what she wanted, no needed and Z was merciless. "Enough," she half breathed half sighed. His response was to use his tongue like a phallus and began to stroke in and out then sliding it up through her folds almost to her clit and back down again. She came again, this time almost twisting off the counter. More irritated than anything, Z slid back from his feast and grabbed Del's arm. Thinking that he was going to help her sit up, Del slowly rose. To her surprise and consternation, he did help her alright, right across his shoulder in a fireman's carry and walked with her over his shoulder right into his bedroom dumping her on the bed.

Del was too amazed at his strength to move for a few moments. She was a solid 215 and floated to 225 during the winter months but at 5'10 most of the weight she carried were in her hips, thighs and breast. Coming back to herself, Del opened her mouth to protest, but looking at her Tarzan she quickly changed her mind. She knew her lover and right now, his mind was on a single track. Due to a whole bunch of reasons, they had not been intimate in a while. Simply put, life had gotten in the way. With Z traveling and Del getting settled in Kannapolis and trying to figure out what was next after her retirement from the military, they kept missing each other. The mini vacation was planned to be the time when they rekindled their relationship. Del had torpedoed that with one look and one touch, but that was the nature of their relationship.

Sliding back on the bed and getting comfortable, Del watched as Z made short work taking his clothes off. Dick swinging, he leaned across the king-sized bed and grabbed Del's ankle. Giggling like she had lost her mind, Del slid face down ass up to the edge of the bed. The giggling stopped as soon as he raised her ass up and smacked it... hard!

In her mind, the sound was still reverberating around the room as she came with the force of a freight train and he entered her from behind. Slow and easy, making sure that his dick rubbed against the already worried clit causing Del to wail pitifully as the orgasm began to build again. He was methodical holding her at the waist and stroking with such tender care. That's how he loved her, as if she was the most precious thing in the world. In this position she was vulnerable, but he didn't use his girth to punish her, rather leveraged it to give his lover as much pleasure as possible. Abruptly, he bent at the waist, maneuvering them both to the bed, with both of them on their sides with Del facing away from him.

With one arm around her chest, he took her leg and placed it over his thigh. Using his hand, he guided his engorged dick into her honey pot causing another moan to escape from Del's parted lips. Del just couldn't help it! She felt every inch of that blessed phallus right to the edge of pain. He covered her from head to toe. In that moment Del couldn't remember a time when she felt so protected, so loved by any lover she ever had. It was in this moment Z made his desires known. Shifting slightly so that he could be closer to her ear he breathed and said, "You were made for me. Don't ever leave me again!"

As soon as the words left his lips, several things happened to emphasize that Z meant every syllable that he spoke. Z stroked up hard and squeezed her nipple with the arm that was wrapped around her. With his other hand he snaked between her legs massaging her clit in time to his stroke. It was too much for Del to handle. Her mind blanked out and she screamed until her voice became horse. Meanwhile Z just continued to stroke powerfully into the woman he loved making sure she understood just how much he missed her.

CHAPTER 14

Baby Girl

It took everything in him not to just show up on her doorstep. It would probably freak her out, but he didn't care. He needed to see his sister! He always felt that she was close, but this was almost too much to bear! Gazing at the picture, Zaire walked away from his computer attempting to tamp down his emotions. She was the splitting image of their mother and from what he had read in the documents he received; she was just as formidable.

Zaire moved round the room towards the sliding glass doors that connected to the deck outside his main bedroom. The house itself sat on roughly five acres that back up to a land conservancy of over three hundred acres. A small creek represented the border between the land conservancy and his property.

Stepping out onto his deck, he breathed in the fresh air. Looking up to the heavens it was a clear night. The stars were bright and what he saw shook him. Pleiades or the seven sisters was clearly visible, reminding him of the oath he had taken. It was one of the reasons he had settled in Huntersville. Time was moving and he wanted to be close to the epicenter as possible. What he was surprised was that his sister was right there in the midst.

The baby girl that he loved with all his heart was so close yet so far away. He always felt a pull to this area which is why he bought the property. The fact that it was surrounded by woods was a bonus.

Where his heart really lied though was the horses. Zaire ran a livery of sorts, taking in large breed older and abused horses making sure that their last days were there best days. Most were draft horses of various breeds with one or two Clydesdales thrown in for good measure. When he was having a tough day, he'd come out to the balcony and gaze out over the pasture, watching them graze and meander around at peace, safe from all hurt, harm, and danger. He was thankful that he could provide them a safe haven. That was one of the things he regretted about his baby sister.

From the data he was able to receive, it appeared that she had a good life, one that was filled with love from two great parents. Baby girl also had a stellar military career which begged the question of why she retired so early – with full benefits. Whatever she did while serving had to be serious. Taking his phone from his pocket, Zaire gazed at the woman who was a replica of his mother. They favored each other so much it was almost scary. Her eyes held so much strength. Gazing back up at the Taurus constellation, Zaire felt the gut kick again. Something was coming and whatever it was, it was not friendly. For sure he needed to make a run. He knew just the spot he could get the information he was looking for.

If Del was a smoker, she'd have a cigarette dragging the hell out of that bitch right now. Fernando had done exactly what she knew he would, make her forget – even if just for a little while. She watched him now, feeling like a perv as he slept peacefully. He was so beautiful and not because his physical appearance. It was his spirit she fell in love with.

Not quite as short as his cousin Invictus, but slightly shorter than Kedar's 6'5 height, Fernando was still impressive in build. If his grandfather Zebulon was any indication of how he was going to age, then he was going to make some woman very happy. Del just wasn't quite sure it was going to be her.

With no sign of her clothes in sight, Del headed to Fernando's closet where she knew she'd find a tank or something to slip on. What she didn't expect to find was so many pairs of Converses… in every color possible. The man she loved was a shoe whore. Giggling out loud, Del made her way to the drawer in the huge closet where she guessed Fernando kept his tanks and shorts grabbed a Nike shirt instead that for sure he would never get back. Checking back in on Fernando who was still sleeping, Del used this small bit of free time to do what the military paid her quite nicely to do, be nosey.

The condo was nothing short of spectacular. It had to span at least three thousand feet, complete with a workout room, an office and well, Del wasn't sure? Cutting on the light, she walked into the room and paused and sheer delight. He is trying to make me love him!! It was a Control Center of sorts. Del could see there were seven thirty-inch monitors stacked by three then by four. If she was able to look at the towers that ran the system, she would weep with joy at the processing speed. The room was painted in a pale lilac and trimmed in gray. On the wall were pictures of sheros, Xena, Storm, Katherine Hughes, Maxine Waters, Wonder Woman circa 1984 and of course Harley Quinn. All total, this was a geek girl dream.

Del couldn't help herself, she had to kick the tires see just what she was working with. Climbing into the lush purple leather office chair, Del cracked her knuckles and powered up the station. That same chair is where Fernando found her. It was supposed to be a surprise, but he couldn't be mad at her. To watch her work was amazing. Like him, multitasking was equivalent to breathing, something that made her good at what she did.

Ever since that young lady had been found on the Andino property, Del had focused her energy on human trafficking. It was heartbreaking work, but he knew that once Del had her mind set on something, she was hard to deter. She's had more failures than success, but every child saved far outweighed the disappointment.

Spinning on his heel, Fernando headed toward the kitchen. Two hours had passed since her arrival and nothing had gone as planned. It was time to gather himself so that they could at least have a conversation and hopefully some excellent takeout. Coffee first, Thai Taste second and maybe once her belly was full, she was relaxed, they could have the conversation she had been avoiding like a kid getting the measles shot.

Undisputed, Edith's was the place to be when you needed either a good meal or information and quite honestly, Zaire was in need of both. Nodding to Matthias as he entered, he made his way to the rear of the small café where the bank of window that faced the street. The universe must have been aligned because the person he wanted to speak to was in a booth that he just passed, but that conversation would need to wait. He would be all kinds of dickhead if he disturbed someone's date. So, he did the next best thing, pressed his way to his seat and tried to figure out exactly what he was going to order.

Zaire watched the couple discreetly or rather watched his friend. The young lady he was with was actually obscured by his hulking figure. Matthias slid up to the table with pad and pencil in hand breaking his vision.

"Long time no see stranger. What can I start you off with?"

"Working backwards today man, I think I want breakfast. By chance is your mother baking?"

"How'd you guess?"

"Gut instinct?" Zaire cheesed as he let the lie roll off his tongue. He could smell the wonder fruit smells wafting from the kitchen. He just hoped all that breaded goodness hadn't been scooped up by other patrons.

Matthias just shook his head smiling, pencil at the ready on the pad.

"Let me have a spinach omelet with American cheese, mushrooms, bell pepper and onions; a side of liver mush; and I'm praying that your mother has some scones left. I don't care what flavor as long as you still have some of her homemade honey butter."

Still writing, Matthias spoke, "Touch and go on the scone, but I may have a cinnamon bun or two left. With or without pecans?"

"A man after my own heart!" Zaire sighed. "With please, but only if you truly don't have any scones left."

"You got it! Give me about ten minutes." With that Matthias

walked towards the double doors that led to the kitchen to drop the order.

The couple that Zaire was tracking was now standing up. Jaw dropping, Zaire looked on in awe at the lovely young lady with a very mischievous smile. As if sensing someone was watching, she leaned over to his direct line of sight and waved. A light flush began to creep up the side of his face. It had been too many moons to count that he recalled a girl had made him blush. Too embarrassed to stop staring Zaire watched as she leaned in and gave her companion a chaste kiss on the cheek while he held her hand. Zaire couldn't remember a time when a woman looked at him like that.

Grabbing her backpack, she hoisted it up on her shoulder. She was dressed in what looked like medical scrubs so maybe she was on her way to work. Holding out her hand, Zaire watched a piece of candy was placed in her hand and the both broke out laughing.

Pivoting quickly, she made her way towards the door, waving at Matthias who was saying something mumbled through the cook's window as she passed by. Taller than average, her long strides got her to the door fairly quickly.

So, lost in tracking the oddly beautiful woman, Zaire forgot one of the first lessons he learned as a child, never lose sight of your prey or you quickly become what you hunt.

A shadow loomed while he was lost in his thoughts. Looking down, he saw a pair of size sixteen if he had to hazard a guess and had to laugh out loud when the shadow spoke, "Size fourteen thank you very much and what has piqued your interest enough to tear yourself away from those massive horses you tend?"

Standing up and laughing simultaneously, Zaire grasped arms with a man he had known far too many years to count. Idris walked back to his table quickly to grab his coffee, then came back to the booth to sit with a man he hadn't spoken to in person in ages.

Zaire gazed at his friend noting a slight difference in his demeanor. Gone was the serious strictly business Idris and what was replaced was to be determined.

"Mighty bold, aren't you?" Zaire asked.

Idris ducked his head in a way that a young teenager would when being asked about his crush. "I know! I know! I've tried to discourage her, but she is as stubborn as her mother and grandmother for that matter."

Both men sat silent for a moment, letting the words that Idris spoke sink in.

"So, what are you going to do?"

"Hope she loses interest?" Idris said hopefully.

"Ummmm Nah, that ain't gonna happen!"

"I know and I can honestly say that I am scared as hell!" Idris took the cup of coffee raising it to his lips for a sip.

"Have you talked to her grandmother?"

"Hell, she's encouraging it! She said that her girls need all the protection that they can get, and the old rules didn't help her daughter in the end."

"You know the boss is not going to like this!" Zaire said with a stern look on his face.

Shrugging his shoulders, Idris stated the obvious, "Who are you most afraid of?"

Hands down Honey Altman along with her brother were a force of nature. Idris along with several other were a part of an elite security team tasked to watch over the siblings and cousin. For the longest time everything had been quiet, but now…

"Can you feel it?" Zaire asked watching Matthias make his way toward the booth with arms full of food.

Matthias deposited the food on the table in quick succession complete with the homemade cinnamon bun with pecans. "I boxed you up a scone to go because I just took these buns out of the oven. I figured you'd love a hot fresh baked bun dripping with icing versus a scone that was made this morning."

Grinning from ear to ear at the feast that was laid before him, "You would be correct! May the Maker shine on you!"

Sliding a second Cinnabon towards Idris, Matthias intoned, "On the house. Can't have you two turning over tables fighting over my mother's baking."

Idris nodded in all seriousness, "And you would be correct." Grabbing the carafe from a nearby station, Matthias filled both their cups with coffee before taking his leave to tend to the other patrons in the café.

"Now tell me old friend, what brings you in town today?" Idris inquired while taking a spoonful of the delicious baked treat up close to his mouth and blowing on it. Sure, he could have used a fork, but why run the risk of dropping any of that velvety smoothness.

"I found my sister." Zaire exclaimed, looking up at Idris with excitement all over his face.

"Do you know how long I have been searching for her, and she was so close all this time?"

Scraping the icing that had begun to pool on the side of the plate Idris asked, "Have you made contact with her yet?"

"Yeah, I sent her a letter and part of her inheritance. I'm trying to be patient and not just pop up on her doorstep. I don't think that

Honey will take kindly to just showing up near her property."

"Wait what?"

"My sister, she lives on a property that is bordered by Honey's."

"Placing his spoon down, Idris looked up at his friend. You don't mean Adelinda?"

"You have seen my sister?"

"In passing, but we have never officially met. How could I miss that! She is the spitting image of your mother!"

Hearing that made Zaire smile. He missed his mother more than he could ever say. Knowing that a part of her visage lived on in the form of his baby sister made his heart happy.

"Well, let me know if you need me to go with you. That's a heavy weight to carry."

"Thanks man! Preciate that. I can reciprocate if you ever want to meet up with your family."

"I'm good on family for right now Idris said quickly, then changing the subject.

"Do you feel a little antsy, like something is coming and it ain't just the rain forecasted for this week?"

"Absolutely. It's part of the reason I'm here. We need to beef up security. You and I are seasoned, but I would rather not rely on our confidence."

"I've been wrestling with the same thought in my mind. Whatever it is, it won't show itself until it's ready. In the meantime, we have bigger fish to fry. Once you reunite with your sister and your mind is more focused, we can talk about changes to the current security set up for the Altman girls."

CHAPTER 15

The Set Up

Jamison set in the office but just couldn't understand what they were asking him to do, or rather why an attorney's office would ask him to do it.

"So, you want me to just keep tabs on her right?"

"Yes of course. Just let us know where she goes and who she sees and report back on a daily basis. Simple."
It still just didn't sit right. Why would a wealthy firm like this who surely had a bank of private eyes that did that sort of work for a living want him to spy on this woman.

The Crocodile, as Jamison had begun to refer to him as had said nothing the entire time. Just sat there grinning and nodding his head as his boss spoke.

"Our sources state that she is supposed to be taking a short trip in roughly three days. We need you to track down the flight plan and beat her there. Once there, our team will take care of the rest."

"Why this girl though?" Jamison wondered out loud, knowing that neither of them would answer.

"Unfortunately, Mr. Hewson, that is above your paygrade. Do we have an agreement?"

Jamison knew in his heart he had done way worse, but he felt like this was a trap. The sad thing was he was already legally obligated

to these bastards by the contract that he singed. Wanting to make sure that there were no cobwebs hanging that he could not see, he asked a clarifying question.
“Once this request is completed it signifies the completion of our signed contract, correct?”

Absolutely, they both said jointly causing Jamison again to look at them suspiciously. He was out of options, but still had one additional question. “You know my freedom still hangs on the word of my bitch ass cousin? What are your current plans to keep me out of harm’s way from that perspective?”

“No love lost huh?”

“Not when it comes to my freedom or his.”

“I see.”

“Your cousin, when the time comes will do as he is told. For now, you need to focus on the task ahead.”

“While I appreciate your confidence, that’s not really addressing my question,” Jamison said pointedly.

“Yours in not to question why. Yours is just to do or die!” This was said with a smile, but Jamison felt it in his very bones.

Nothing here was as it appeared, and he knew just like his very next breath, his days were numbered.

Cassius sat on the deck of his parent’s house and watched nothing and everything. His mind could not register that he was free, at least for the time being. His parents really didn’t say much to him and that was fine because he really didn’t have much to say.

The one person that he desperately wanted to hear from refused to return his call. Nora refused to talk to him. The woman that he loved with all his heart and did all the things he could possibly do to make sure she was happy won’t even give him the time of day.

He knew who to blame. It was all Asa's fault. If she had just kept the ring, none of this would have happened.

It was a refrain that he repeated over and over in his mind. Nothing for him would change the fact that fat bitch ruined his life. If he could just talk to Nora, he could make her understand. He didn't care that she had a daughter. They could be a family together. He just wanted to see her; to touch her again.

"Cassius?" His mother call inquiring where he was. It wasn't like he had a broke him from his only slice of happiness right now in his life, planning how he would get the love of his life back.

"Your legal team is here to see you." She said smiling with pride shining through her voice. It took everything that he had not to say anything. They, his parents let him sit in that jail and rot. If it wasn't for his public defender, he would be dead now, but she confused him with his words – legal team?

Now curious, Cassius stood up and headed towards the door that would lead him to the kitchen. His mother stopped him holding a tray of hot tea, milk, sugar and finger sandwiches. Standing to the side, but holding the door, he let her walk out to the enclosed deck. Behind her were the members of the legal team. Cassius looked on slightly confused.

"Good Afternoon Mr. Hewson!"

Holding his hand out, he grabbed hers almost reverently. If not for this woman, he would still be rotting in jail. "Attorney Young! I wasn't expecting to see you. I didn't realize that we had a scheduled meeting, or I would have been dressed." Cassius still had on his pajamas and had not showered. It wasn't like he was going to have visitors and he normally just took a shower before he went to bed.

"Well, there's been some changes in your defense, and I wanted to address them with you in person. Let me introduce you to my new employer, Attorney C. Redrosid. He is one of the managing partners of the Firm Redrosid, Maldeb, and Roth. They are a small firm that only takes on very high-profile clients. They offered me a position, and I took their offer only with the understanding that your case would be coming with me."

Dumbstruck at her kindness, Cassius had a moment of elation, then crashed back to the ground. He had no money so there was no way that he could possibly afford a firm of the caliber she was describing. It was then that the man that entered with her spoke.

"I sssee the look of ssurprise on your face Mr. Hewson. But don't concern yourself. We have approved this request and will be taking on your casssse."

Cassius tried not to stare but couldn't help it. The man was, well he was complex. First off, he had the most beautiful eyes he had ever seen. They were almost the color of moss with flecks of green interchanged with brown. He was tall, about the average size of an NFL running back and built like one. Cassius could see that through the well fitted suit. His voice though? It was not quite stuttering but like he held on to the S just a little too long. It wasn't on every word that contained an s, just every so often. It was still weird. His mother cleared her throat, breaking the almost trance like gaze Mr. Redrosid held him under.

"Sir, I can't begin to thank you for your kindness," Cassius said quickly remembering his manners.

His attorney jumped in redirecting his attention, "No thanks necessary. Besides, you are innocent and call me Jez. You and I will be spending a lot of time together over the next few weeks while we try to get these charges dismissed. But for now, we need you to tell us all the players that were a part of your afterhours club. From what we read via the police reports, Jamison Hewson was courting BCI more specifically, Invictus LeBlanc. Is this true?"

Cassius began to panic, remembering clearly what the White Rose made plain. So, he did what he was told, "I sent out invitations to all my associates of means and Mr. LeBlanc is one of them. It was Jamison Hewson who both helped finance and provided the ladies. They were supposed to be hostesses, not sex slaves. I had no idea that any of them were underage or that they were stolen from their families.

Finishing his statement, Cassius looked over at his mother to gage her reaction and she looked mortified. It was what he intended his statement to be. He wanted to hurt her anyway possible. She needed to understand the hell he had been through over the last couple of months.

Cassius could hear Jez's pen scratching and he knew, based on the numbers churning on her phone that voice dictation was being taken as well.

Is there a reason why you transferred several properties without any cash being moved to BCI international?

"Unfortunately, Lady Luck was not on my side the last time we had a game night and I had to leverage my properties to settle the debt." Cassius looked embarrassed which was an honest emotion right now as he thought about how the White Rose kept drilling him on his actions or lack thereof.

Mr. Redrosid never spoke, but Cassius could feel his eyes taking in every detail of his moment. Then he felt it, like a light feathery touch sliding down the nape of his neck. It made him shiver.

Pulling his attention away from Jez, he looked up to meet Mr. Redrosid's eyes. There was something not quite right about his eyes.

"Well Cassius I think that we have what we need," Jez said unknowingly breaking the tension in the room. Even Cassius's mother was squirming just a little and the way that Mr. Redrosid was eyeing her son. She knew a predator when she saw one.

"Please let us know immediately if your cousin tries to reach out to either of you." Jez said looking at both Cassius and his mother.

Both quickly nodded in agreement. Breaking her silence, Mrs. Hewson stood and said overly loud, "Let me show you to the front."

Holding out her hand directing them to a path the ran around the side of the house. The quickest way between two points was a straight line and she wanted this man off her property as soon as humanly possible.

A few minutes passed and she came back through the house looking for her son. Not the sharpest tool in the shed considering the recent mistakes he had made, but as a mother she could not keep quiet.

"Son while you may hate your father and I right now because we didn't originally run to your defense, I need you to listen very closely to me. That man walks with death. Do not cross him. Whatever you need to do to satisfy the requirements of your agreement you do and be done with them."

With that said she turned and walked back into the house, leaving her tea set and the remaining sandwiches outside she was so shaken. The fact that she wasn't rushing to clean up the table told Cassius just how bothered his mother was about that man's presence. She wasn't alone in her thinking. The sooner he could get this case cleared, the sooner he could be free. While normally he would disagree just to be arbitrary, his mother was right. That man was creepy as hell.

CHAPTER 16

Second Thoughts

Zalmon stood looking out the window, but really looking at nothing at all. Simply put he was too angry to look at anything. In a word, he was fucked. Thanks to his greedy son, they both had been basically removed from the line of succession. While his background was not necessarily squeaky clean, he never stooped that low to make some cash. As usual, his mother's recon was flawless, complete with pictures. Zalmon even had his on actuary to run the numbers and they all came out the same.

To Zalmon's thinking, his mother was right on two accounts: his son was guilty as hell; and he didn't deserve to run the corporation – or rather couldn't afford to run the corporation. It would only take one of those victims to step forward and identify his son as being present and that would be that. Now they had to clean up the mess. Each of these little girls or boys would have to be tracked down and compensated with a nondisclosure. His mother was right, they owed them that much. Which is why he also now understood the numbers his mother was requesting and would no longer argue.

He did have other options. He could try to have more children which wouldn't be a hardship. Or he could focus on the child that he had. As much as he didn't want to admit it, Fernando more than likely was his son. It wasn't something he was proud of, the treatment of his mother that is, but there was nothing that he could do to change the past. Walking back to his desk, he picked up the picture that his assistant had sent him. On his desk was a picture of his father's mother and placed side by side, the two looked like twins instead of great-grandson and great-grandfather.

Sighing, Zalmon knew that Vic's bridges were all but burnt. He would always have a place at BCI, but it would never be at the helm. There was one thing that bothered him though? Exactly how much did his father know about his oldest son? There was only one way to find out and this was a conversation best held in person.

“Ariana?” Zalmon called distractedly. “Please book me a flight home and make sure that my father is in residence.”

Placing both pictures down, Zalmon sat back in his chair. There was more to this situation that met the eye. Talking to his father was a starting place, but he knew in his gut, there was way more that was about to be uncovered.

Fernando and Del sat at his kitchen table and ate like hostages that hadn’t been feed in weeks. Thai Basil hands down had some of the best food in Charlotte. They had everything from Pad Thai to spring rolls, to Tom Yum soup. Fernando and Del ate in companionable silence listening to Charlie Wilson’s Outstanding, both bobbing their heads at the appropriate time.

It was at the bridge when the bongos where drilling out the rhythm when Del found the courage to tell Z her truth.

“I have a brother.”

“I know.”

The music faded and Del dropped her chopsticks on the table. Maybe he didn’t hear what she said so she tried again. “I said, I have a brother.”

As if he was discussing a butterfly on a leaf, Z treated one of the most significant moments in her life like it was nothing. Not understanding the storm that was brewing, he continued with his explanation, “I know. He contacted me a few weeks back. Said that he wanted to meet you. I was trying to run it down before I said anything to you.”

The fact that he was trying to run it down did take some of the sting off his delivery, but it still left a sour taste in her mouth.

Pushing her chair away from the table, Del decided it was time to leave before she said something that she couldn't take back. Z realizing too late the mood of his lover, placed the napkin in his lap on the table and followed quickly behind her, grabbing her on the shoulder in an attempt to slow her down. Maybe he forgot that she was a Marine or that she hated to be grabbed from behind. Or maybe he thought he could still man handle her like he did earlier with the wonderful bed play they had. That was then and this is now – and right now Del was pissed!

First grabbing his wrist, she pulled his arm forward. Smiling, thinking that she wasn't mad. Z let her pull his arm forward without resistance. Using the strength of her legs, Del dropped down, continuing to pull him forward and then powered up thankful for the workout she had done twice a week with Charleston. Del heard his shoulder pop or maybe it was his back? Either way he went flying – over her shoulder and on to the table.

"Don't touch me!" It was said calmly. Too calmly, but Z just had the wind knocked out of him, so he was really trying to focus on just breathing.

"Shit you could have said that before you threw my black ass across the room," Z moaned as he laid prostrate across a thick wooden table.

Ignoring his pitiful groan, Del walked into the master suite and changed her clothes.

"So, I guess this mean you're mad at me?" Z shouted still flat on his back on the hard-wooden table.

On her way back into the room with her overnight bag, she pulled his hair.

"Oooowwww! Now that was low and uncalled for!" he whined again. Z laid there trying to figure out what went wrong. He knew that she wasn't weak, but damn! She knocked a pause in him. Opening the door Del stood face to face with Kedar who was about to knock. Giving him a once over she snarled, "Punks jump up to get beat down!"

Looking confused, Kedar suggested, "Brand Nubians?"
Still laying on the table, Z hollered from the room, "You better be at the airport on Saturday! I'm not playing with you Adelinda!" Kedar watched as Del said nothing but flipped his cousin the bird in the general direction where his cousin's voice resonated from. She said nothing as she walked out the door and headed toward the elevator. Not seeing his cousin, Kedar let himself in and called his name.

"In here," came the weak response.

Kedar walked into the family, but still didn't see his cousin, that is until he looked down at the table. There his cousin lay, sprawled haphazardly apparently where his paramour left him.

"She just whopped your ass, didn't she?"

"Like a rented mule."

"What'd you do."

"Nothin." Holding his hand out, Kedar tried to assist his cousin,

"What did you do?"

Z grunted as begrudgingly accepted his cousin's hand who unceremoniously jacked him off the table. Side eyeing his cousin and trying to sidestep the question, "Boy you are strong like an ox! When's the last time you dabbled?"

With the same look his grandfather Zebulon gave when he meant business, Kedar just stared at his cousin awaiting his response. Ever since Kedar had is his heart broken with Asa, he had been way more serious. Z struggled with his fledgling relationship with Del, so for sure he had no advice to give. Meanwhile Kedar continued to stare, waiting on his response.

“Apparently she didn’t appreciate me being helpful,” Z snapped trying to put his hair back up into the bun it had fallen out of.

Closing his eyes in a fervent plea to the heavens, “Please tell me you let her know about the man claiming to be her brother?”
Z tried to look innocent, but it was an epic failure. Kedar shook his head and walked back towards the kitchen. He smelled food and didn’t have time to eat while he was traveling back to the Carolinas. He was on one call after the next and Z was not picking up his phone. He now understood why.

Z came into the kitchen area rotating his shoulder and stretching his back. Kedar snorted, “You’re lucky she didn’t snap your neck! What were you thinking? She should have whooped your ass! You’re damn lucky she didn’t put any hot shit in ya!”

Z moved around to the bar and poured himself a shot of Don Julio. Starring at his cousin, he waited for the lecture to continue. But he was surprised, Kedar took off his suit coat and rolled up his sleeves to wash his hands.

“Thai Basil?”

Z nodded and watched while his cousin fixed himself a plate and grabbed a spring roll. No other words were spoken as Kedar dug into what should have been his romantic meal with Del. Minutes passed while the cousins sat in relative silence, with only the soundtrack playing in the background. The player switched over Jennifer Hudson’s version of Golden Slumbers and Kedar looked up mid-chew with and eyebrow raised.

“Why are you here?” Z deflected. He was contemplating putting on his clothes and tracking Del down. She owed him and apology and damnit, he was not going to leave her alone until he got one!

“Because you don’t answer a phone! Tweedledee and Tweedledumb are out of jail. Both have been bonded out by very prestigious law firms. While I’m not worried that any roads will lead back to us, your "faaaasher" mimicking Dr. Evil, will probably do something stupid." Looking around the table for something to drink and finding none, Kedar went to the pantry and pulled out a Nehi Peach in a glass bottle. Taking the cap off, he grabbed a napkin and returned to the table.

Pushing off the counter he was leaning on, Z walked back to his playroom and did what he did best, seek information. Anything was better than thinking about the fact that Zalmon LeBlanc was his father and Vic was his dickhead little brother. Quite honestly, Z could give a rat's ass about what happened to either of them. What concerned him was the series of events. The fact that a random has come up looking for Del and now these idiots are out on bond. Knowing his Kedar like it did, for sure there was already a tail on both, but Z wanted to know more about the firms that were representing them. What did they have to gain?

Cranking up his network, Z decided to grab his laptop instead and bring it back to the table where Kedar was eating the last of what should have been a romantic dinner between he and Del. He worked in silence, well with the exception of Kedar's grunting every now and then over exactly how good the Tom Kah was, then he found it. Shit!

Kedar broke from his love affair with the food long enough to wipe his hands and come over to his side of the table.

"The White Rose is not going to be happy at all," Kedar mumbled, taking a bite out of the fried shrimp wrap.

"Yeah, this is interesting don't you think? The same law firm that represented the dude that wanted to purchase a stake in our company is now representing child traffickers."

"The better question is, who is going to tell her?" Kedar asked suspiciously.

"Rock, Paper, Scissors, Lizard, Spock?" Z declared, confident that he would not end up on the short end of the stick.

CHAPTER 17

Off the Grid

They controlled everything from the phone I used to the condo in which I now reside. This is not right! That refrain kept rolling around in his head the entire ride to his new home. Jamison was still dazed and confused as he stepped out of the car that dropped him off at his new home. They kept saying it was for his own protection, at least until the business with his cousin could be resolved.

Jamison took the eight by eleven brown envelope and followed the new watchdog that escorted him to the door. Key in his hand he unlocked the door to his new digs. Stepping through the doorway, Jamison had to hide his shock. This was not what he expected, not at all. Even if he had money like this, he would never roll like this. All of this luxury had to be running the firm at least two bands a month and that wasn't even taking the utilities into consideration.

"Here's the laptop, three thousand in cash, and your set of keys to the condo. You have the cell phone," he nodded looking down to Jamison's hand. "It should be on at all times. As for transportation, you need none. You are on call twenty-four by seven or until your contract is notified. You need to stay off the grid so no bank transactions or card usage. Any issues come up just call Doc and he will get it sorted out."

Jamison had not paid much attention to the phone since he received it with everything else going on. Unlocking the phone, he brought up his contact list and sure enough, there was an entry for Doc.

Still trying to wear the mask, Jamison looked up at his new prison guard and nodded that he understood. "My name is Sir. I'll be your point of contact going forward. Within one block of this residence are seven different restaurants and a small grocery store. Make it work. I don't need to tell you that you are to contact no one until your contract is fulfilled."

Even if Jamison did want to talk to someone, no one would believe him. So, he just nodded his agreement.

"You have the look of self-preservation about you. I suggest you take this seriously." With that said, there was no waiting for a response. Sir just walked out the door. Jamison stood, watching the door close silently and tried to rationalize everything that had happened today and failed… miserably. There was nothing to do now but wait. Exploring his new home, Jamison walked down the hallway peeking it what appeared to be a guest room and a hall bathroom. At the end of the all was a closed door. Curious to see what he had truly gotten himself into, he pushed the door open slowly.

To his shock the room was completely filled with his belongings. They had somehow gotten into the home that he had previously rented before he was arrested and gathered his things. The keys to the car he had purchased were sitting on the dresser. Grabbing the keys, he thought for a moment about heading down to the garage to see if it was parked there. Even if it was, Jamison was sure that it was now being tracked so why tempt fate?

Pulling open the dresser draw he picked up new socks and underwear that had been neatly folded, alongside the old things he had owned before. Stumbling back, his leg hit the footboard and he pitched backwards landing on the bed. Too overwhelmed with fear, Jamison used both hands to cover his face. He laid there immobile with reality crashing down on him. There was no doubt in his mind now that he was effectively off the grid. At any moment they could snuff his ass out and nobody would know, in effect he had been ghosted.

It was in that very moment that Jamison knew with all his heart his chances of survival were slim to none. Even if he did what that wanted him to do to the letter, he was going to die. There was nothing else to do but try to get some rest, so he pulled his shoes off and stretched out across the bed. It took a while, but finally he settled into a restless sleep. He dreamed. In his dreams he was in a field and he was surrounded by eyes that were reflecting light. He could hear a growl but couldn't see what body was attached to the eyes. Drifting from the sky were feathers made of iridescent colors of purple, black, and gold. There was a tree not far away and in it he could see a beautiful bird. It reminded him of a peacock, but the colors were in the spectrum of flames, white, yellow, red and finally blue. While the bird was illuminated, the limb that she was resting on didn't burn. He didn't really know what sex it was, it just felt like feminine energy pouring out. The voice when it issued sounded like a thousand voices each saying the same thing, death.

Jamison felt pain and touched his hand to his neck. Waking up with a scream and swinging his harms at a paltry attempt to protect himself. Flat on his back, he held his hand in the air, trying to catch the last light of the fading sun. There it was, plain as day – blood. Jumping up from the bed Jamison ran to the bathroom to look at himself in the mirror. His neck was intact, with not a scratch but his hand, was covered in blood. Scrambling now, Jamison struggled to cut the faucet on because his hands were slick with blood. He finally succeeded, watching the water go from crimson, to pink to clear.

Holding his blood free hand up again to check for injury, Jamison couldn't find one. He heard it again – "Death."

Sliding down to the floor, Jamison did something he hadn't done since he was a little boy; he wept. He knew as sure as he was born what he had just dreamt was his death.

CHAPTER 18

Sorrow

Years of honing her instincts in the Marines for way too many years to count should prepared her for this moment. Breathing deeply, she cut the car off. It was at that moment that the phone rang.

"You know you owe me, right?" Del exhaled picking up the phone in the car so that she could talk to the object of her current frustration.

Charleston tried to contain his laughter but failed miserably. "It's just a swim lesson. You got this. All Asa needs you to do is to watch her while she runs to speak with her agent. There is some type of emergency with her next expo. She just needs to get to a quiet place so that they can facetime."

"You better be glad I love my niece! You know kids don't like me!"

"Most, but not all. The twins and Charlie love you. Plus, you know that Z will eventually want a family. This is the best way to get some practice in."

Breathing deeply, Del had to gather herself. He was her best friend on the planet – so yeah, he would have guessed the one thing that scared the shit out of her, though not the true root cause. Leaning her had back against the seat, Del breathed deep. Tears began to gather at the thought, and she clasped the small sachet she kept around her neck. Inside the sachet was the greatest gift she ever created, her son.

Z never knew the reason why she left and truthfully, it was a pain that she struggled with every day. She never wore the sachet when she was in his presence, which until lately was not very often. She had no clue she was pregnant and didn't have any of the traditional illnesses associated with being pregnant. Her periods were never regular, and it wasn't until the debilitating cramps started that she knew something was horribly wrong. Tears gathered in her eyes thinking about the loss. It was like a piece of her was missing and she didn't know how to make it right.

According to the attending OBGYN, she was roughly eleven weeks along. Her son was perfectly formed and a little fighter, but there was no way he could have survived outside the womb. She had his remains converted into a diamond. Tears that had gathered were now falling and Del willingly gave in to the sorrow – it was the only way to keep herself sane.

The phone rang breaking her moment of mourning. Asa was in a bit of a panic if she was calling right after Charleston.

"Del? Thank you so much for helping out. Charlie only has about forty-five minutes left. This call should only take about thirty." Tamping down her emotions Del cleared her throat, "I just parked. I'm walking in right now."

Del pulled the visor down to check her face and took a deep breath. Making sure her sachet was nestled down next to her heart.

Jamison sat in the car with Sir and knew that time was running out.

"We need to grab her now!" an anxious Jamison pushed.

"If you want to go back to jail… sure." Sir stated calmly. "Don't you see the cameras on the side of the building? This ain't your little sex trafficking ring junior."

Looking at the surrounding buildings, Jamison belatedly noticed the cameras. Sir was right, his ass would have been right back in jail. He just wanted this over. He was worried about what the LeBlanc's would do to him if they caught up to him, but his attorney – she truly scared him. If he ran, they were going to kill him, of that he had no doubt.

“We’ll just follow her back to the property and snatch her there.” Sir made it sound all simple, like breathing. Jamison felt it in his bones that this was dumb as hell, but what could he say? Looking at his jailor, “Whatever you say boss.”

Leaning back in his seat, Jamison closed his eyes. He had no idea when he would be able to get any rest again.

“I know, I know, I know, I know… that I aught to leave the young thang alone, but ain’t no sunshine when she’s gone.” Sang sweetly word for word by someone who was struggling to tie her shoes.

Del just shook her head and smiled. Charlie knew all the words to Bill Withers and sang it with a passion. Forty-five minutes turned into, let me put the car seat in your car because I need to run over to the venue. That’s how Del and Charlie ended up on their way back home after her swim class.

Del had to admit her niece was a surprisingly a good swimmer, like in a few years she needed to be on someone’s junior Olympic team swimmer. She was amazing to watch, learning strokes and styles that she as an adult couldn’t even master, and her singing voice wasn’t that shabby either. Laughing out loud at her thoughts caught Charlie’s attention.

“Auntie D?”

“Yes Baby?”

“Why were you so sad today?” Her question took Del back. She was just laughing a second ago so why would Charlie think she was sad?

“Auntie Del wasn’t sad sweetheart …”

“Yes, you were, you were sad about him. Why?”

Beginning to be freaked out because this was such a weird

conversation to have with one so young. Nervous about where the conversation was going, Del checked her rearview mirror and noticed a car following a hundred yard back or so. Del's eyes shifted back towards her passenger then back to the road. They were almost home, maybe a mile away from onto the drive that led to the house.

"He's okay though," Charlie went on to say thoughtfully. "He just hates to see you cry, like you were doing before you came to get me."

Del's heart skipped a beat and her attention snatched from the road to look at Charlie again. How in the world did Charlie know she had been crying?

"He wuvs you very much Auntie Del and wishes you wouldn't cry," Charlie added sadly.

At that moment Del couldn't take her eyes off of Charlie. Maybe if she had, she would have seen the car that was once a hundred yards off literally on her bumper, but had cut their headlights and the car that was well ahead of her had come to a complete unexpected stop. Immediately, her instinct kicked in, but not in enough time to break without tapping the rear of the car in front of her. The car behind her must have been following close, because they screeched to a halt at an angle, effectively trapping her between the two cars.

"Baby Girl? Are you okay?" Del asked shaken.

The response was laughter, "Do it again! Do it again!"
Shaking her head, Del whipped out her phone to call in the accident. She was on the line with 911when the passenger from the car behind approached her from the rear of the car. Rolling her window down enough to hear him, with the dispatcher on Bluetooth, Del asked, "Are you hurt sir?"

Because she had the baby in the car, there was no way she would get out and leave little Charlie unprotected until either Charleston or someone in the immediate family arrived.

“No, but I think I may have scratched your car. You may want to hop out and take a look.”

“I’ll just wait till the police arrive,” Dell said suspiciously. She always kept a weapon in the car and this man lurking was making her palm itchy.

The person she tapped was now out of the car and Del didn’t like this one bit. She looked back at Charlie who didn’t have a care in the world. She had her tablet out and had put on her headphones.

Del was still was giving the dispatcher the address so that they could get there as quickly as possible. The phone was ringing for Charleston when the man approached the car again.

“You need to get out of the car and check the damages ma’am,” he said, borderline aggressive.

Charleston had just picked up the phone, so Del ignored the man and began to roll up the window. “Hey Charleston!”

But it wasn’t Charleston, it was Christopher who picked up the phone. “Hey Adelinda! Charleston told me to grab the phone.”

“Hey Chris – Look I’m about five minutes from the house and have gotten into a little fender bender. I need Charleston to come and pick Charlie up so that I can take care of the report with the officer when they arrive. I’m probably a half a mile off the turn from Highway 3.”

“Are you okay?” Christopher asked concerned. Del could hear him moving and dogs yipping in the background as if something was wrong. Maybe they sensed his distress. She could hear Christopher calling for Charleston and stating that he was placing the phone on speaker.

A tap sounded at her window, one that sounded like metal against glass. Distorted through the glass Del heard, "I tried to be nice, but you want to be a stubborn bitch. Get out of the car now and don't try shit!"

Her options were few. If she pulled her weapon, she risked them shooting into the car and harming Charlie. She said it low and quick. "Purple Rain". It was the code that Charleston and Del had set up when they were in the field. It meant that there was trouble or a trap.

Hearing her through the speaker, Charleston responded, "Roger." Now she needed to stall so that either the police or Charleston could get there. Either way, she wanted the danger away from Charlie. The car was an X5 and Del knew that Z's paranoid ass had made sure it was bullet proof, but she still didn't want to take any chances. The windows were tented, so they couldn't tell if there was another passenger in the car. Del could only assume that they had be following her and knew she normally rode alone.

"Look, I don't have any money and this car has a tracking system in it so it can't be stolen," Del listed out the obvious options. There was a total of five men, each had a weapon trained on her as she slowly exited the car. Del kept the door slightly ajar so that Christopher and Charleston could still hear her through the Bluetooth. Keeping her voice overly loud to give Charleston as much description as possible, "Five grown men and two cars to trap me? Why? Did I cut you off in traffic? Surely the dent is not that bad?"

"That's enough conversation ma'am," said the tallest of the crew. We just need a word with you in private. Come quietly and there won't be any issues."

"Honey, you already got issues. I'm the last person you really want to fuck with."

Del said this with a calmness the belied her anger. She hated bullies and these men, were bullies. She looked at each of them and then recognized a familiar face. "Jamison Hewson as I live and breathe, surely you're not hang with this group of misguided gentlemen?"

Jamison swallowed hard but didn't respond. He kept looking around wildly at the trees, almost as if he was hoping to find something. Neither of the drivers of the SUV nor the car got out, they just kept the cars idle which meant they were looking for a quick exit. The question remained for Del was whether she would be alive or dead when they left.

Sucking her teeth in disappointment, "I hope your affairs are in order."

Hands shaking, still looking at the trees and now the sky, Jamison lowered his weapon, attempting to place it in the holster but kept missing it. "She's stalling. Get her in the car but tie her hands! She whopped my cousin's ass without breaking a sweat and she can take a punch."

At that moment a howl rent the air. One of the hired guns yelled,

"What in the world was that?" With a smile of pure hatred, Del calmly declared, "Your death."

Now moving into true panic, Jamison screamed, "Get her in the car now. Those are not dogs; those are wolves and they will kill." Scrambling now to follow through with orders, two of the men lunged at Del to tie her hands, and that is when the fight began.

Rolling forward on the ground Del came back up with a left punch dropping one of the men like a sack of potatoes. The other man was smarter, now circling her drawing her out into the field where the ground as level. Del was trying to get them as far away from the car as possible so that she could keep her charge safe. In the distance another howl could be heard, and desperate Jamison screamed at them again to hurry.

The first shot ricochet near Del's left foot, but she didn't care. She would fight until there was none left in her.

"Shit!" One of the guys hollered. What are those things? Del didn't take her eyes off the fight but realized too late what she didn't do – lock the car.

That momentary thought made her lose focus long enough for one the men to get in a lucky punch that landed on her temple and she went out like a light.

The men stood winded trying to figure out how they almost got their asses handed to them by one lone woman, when another howl reverberated through the air much closer.

"Hurry!" Jamison yelled again.

One man slung Del over his shoulder unceremoniously and dumped her in the trunk. All the attackers piled back into their respective cars or SUV, leaving Del's X5 on the road. Time was of the essence and the police would be there at any minute.

No sooner than they got into their cars, bursting from the woods in the distance was some of the biggest dogs that any of them had ever seen.

Now in full panic Jamison yelled, "Go, Go, Go!!"

The two cars took off leaving Del's car behind racing towards the county line and away from the city. Jamison could see lights flashing in the distance behind them and knew that they moved just in time.

Suddenly the car swerved, almost as if it had hit something with a loud thump coming off the driver's side door. Sir who was driving and never got out of the car blinked twice, believing his eyes were deceiving him. He thought that Jamison was just scary, no… Jamison was a realist. That was an enormous dog that bounced off the door rolled and stood up like it wasn't nothing. There not just one, but an entire pack of them running towards them in the field as they speed past. What the fuck?

“Drive! Drive! Drive!” Jamison screamed. One hand on the wheel and one hand on his face, Sir pushed the pedal to the floor trying to outpace whatever that was, but the image was sealed to his mind.

“Who is this woman?” He asked Jamison.

“Someone I was told not to fuck with – and now you understand why. This is not over! And if you think that all that tight ass security is going to stop these country ass people from getting to you, then you’re crazy as hell!”

Sir gripped the wheel tighter and kept his eyes on the road and his hands at ten and two.

Jamison was never a man for religion but found some of his Catholic training if only for a moment and crossed himself. In his heart he knew this was the beginning of the end.

CHAPTER 19

Moving Heaven and Earth

What should have been a simple traffic incident would undoubtedly become a crime scene. The Cabarrus County Sheriff, along with a State Trooper, met them at Del's X5 parked on the side of the road. Charlene was in the arms of the Trooper and seemed not the worse for wear, but there were no other cars or people in sight. Charleston and Christopher made it to the car first, with Ezra, Idris, and a stranger not far behind.

"Dada!" Charlene screeched with excitement when she saw her Papa. It was the way she always reacted anytime they were apart, whether it was for a short weekend when she went back to stay with her grandmother, or when she was a preschool for the day.

With quick strides, arms held wide, Charleston grabbed his daughter and held her close. It was not that long ago that a threat was in play to snatch his baby girl. Seeing the scene laid out before him was too close for comfort, especially since Del was nowhere to be found. He tried not to think the worst, but doubts continued to creep in this mind.

While Charleston was rocking his daughter, checking her over for any injuries, Christopher kept his eyes on the men approaching so that they could all hear the same story and collectively ask questions. The officers couldn't help but notice how tall and broad the men were, and you could sense their awareness in the way their demeanor changed. They straightened their backs and stood a little taller. Clearing his throat, Trooper Robertson addressed the wall of testosterone, "I take it you're related to this little one?"

Each of the men nodded in turn, even the stranger, but Charleston vocalized explicitly, "This is my daughter. My name is Charleston."

He paused, turning his body in the directions of his home. "My daughter and I live about three-quarters of a mile from here. Her Godmother was bringing her home from swim practice when we got a call that she was in an accident."

Nodding his head and taking notes, Trooper Robertson asked, "Would she have any reason to leave the little girl in the car?"

Not overly fond of being referred to as "little girl," Charlene interjected with a fierce frown, "My name is Charlene, and my Dada's name is Charleston."

Looking at her with a smile, Trooper Robertson apologized, "I'm sorry little one, I meant to say, Charlene."

Huffing just a little, she reluctantly replied, "It's okay." Turning to face to her father, signaling she finished with the conversation with the officer, Charlene focused intently on Charleston and asked,

"Dada? What happened to Auntie Del and the other cars?

Rubbing his daughters back, Charleston posed, "How many cars were there, sweetheart?"

"There were two cars, one in the front and one in back. A mean man kept tapping on the window. I put my headphones on and stayed quiet, but I didn't like him," Charlene finished with a frown.

Realizing his daughter had more to tell, Charleston asked what the Trooper couldn't get her to say. "Okay, kitten, tell Dada everything you saw."

Charlie put her hand over her eyes, almost as if she was trying to block out everything so that she could remember. A short moment passed, and then she spoke, "Two cars, five men, Auntie Del fighting and then a loud pop. Auntie Del went to sleep, and the mean man carried her to the car. Both cars left. Luke opened the door and told me it would be okay and that you would be here in just a second."

Both Charleston and Christopher looked confused, but Ezra, Idris, and the newcomer were looking everywhere but at the officers.

"Charlene? Who is Luke?" Charleston asked calmly.
Ezra piped up before she could answer, "Could a pop mean gunfire?

"Charlie, baby? Did you see a gun?"

Her little eyebrows knitted together once again, "Yes, Dada, all the men had guns, and they were pointing them at Auntie Del."
Sheriff Ford turned to Trooper Roberston and spoke what everyone present accepted as fact, "We need to get the Crime Scene folks out here ASAP!" Walking back to his car, he made the call.

Trooper Roberston stared at Charleston hard for a few minutes before asking, "Sir, before I let you and your daughter go, do you have any identification?"

Irritated, Charleston handed Charlie to Ezra so he could fish his wallet out of his pocket. The officer took the identification and scanned it using his phone. Once satisfied, he gave the license back to Charleston.

"Do you have any idea who would want to kidnap your friend?" There could have been a myriad of people that wanted Del dead based on what they had to do to serve and protect the country they loved. That response would have just added fuel to the fire, so instead, he went with what he was positive about, "No sir, I don't, but if they had the least bit of intelligence, they would let her go unharmed and immediately. Adelinda is a former Marine that's trained with both the Navy and Army Special Forces."

Pausing for a moment, he let that sink in. Pointing to the field behind them, "I'm pretty sure once you get the proper lighting in here, you'll see signs of a fight. The only reason there are no bodies on the ground is that my daughter was in the car. Del wouldn't risk her getting hurt or seeing any more violence than necessary."

Now pointing to the car, Charleston added, "I'm also sure that once you search the car, you'll find her registered weapon.

Both Idris and the stranger had moved away from the group and were speaking amongst themselves, looking at everyone agreed now was a crime scene. The road was now blocked off as officers began to reroute traffic. Ushering Christopher and Ezra over, who was still holding Charlene, Idris pointed to the ground in front of Del's car.

"Looks like they sandwiched her in."

The stranger piped in, "I wonder how long they have been following her? Surely they had to know she wasn't alone - that there was a child in the car?"

"Oh, but they will care," Christopher spat angrily.
Idris cleared his throat and motioned Charleston over so that he

could make the introductions only once. "Everyone, this is Del's brother Zaire. We work for the same security company. Zaire generally takes clients in the Huntersville area."

Turning to look at Zaire, "Zaire - this is Charleston, Del's best friend, and fellow Marine. Charleston is also Savannah's brother is Christopher's fiancé. Of course, you already know Ezra, Christopher's grandfather."

Each man held out a hand to shake Zaire's in kind. The fact that Idris and Zaire knew each other was a question for another time.

Right now, the most important thing was getting Del home. Christopher looked at Charleston thoughtfully, "We need to let Fernando know what's happened."

The men all nodded in agreement, and Christopher whipped out his cell to contact him. Fernando and Christopher had rekindled their childhood friendship during his mother's fiftieth surprise birthday party. The phone rang once, and Fernando picked up. "Hey, man! What's up?"

Not one to mince words, Christopher just cut to the chase, "Del and Charlene were ambushed on the way home from swim practice. Charlene is safe, but Del is missing. We'll be setting up at my house, either waiting on a word from the kidnappers or the detectives."

Sounding way calmer than he should have, "My people are at your disposal. My cousin and I will be there in about forty-five minutes. Is Charlene okay?"

Looking at his good friend and soon to be brother in law, "She's fine. Charleston has her in his arms right now. They hit Del's car about three-quarters of a mile from the house."

Fernando was silent for a beat, "I know you can take care of yourself, but at least let me send some of our security detail." Christopher looked at his grandfather and shook his head, then verbalized, "That won't be necessary, but I do appreciate the offer. See you in forty-five."

"I need to get you home, baby girl, so you can get a bath and get ready for bed." Charleston sighed, hugging his daughter tight, thanking the maker for both her safety and Del's sacrifice.

"But Dada, I'm not sleepy!" Charlene protested. All the men laughed, knowing how it felt to be young and having so much energy.

"How is it you can speak the Queen's English at almost four, but can't say, Daddy?" Charleston asked his now frowning daughter.

"Because you're not my Da-Dee," Charlene said harshly. Pointing at his chest to emphasize her point, "You are my Dada - D A D A." Though she spelled it out, she pronounced it like there was a missing a and an h at the end of the word, Dadaah.
Smile twitching on his lips while the other men look anyway at the now serious and slightly perturbed Charlene, "Noted!"

Christoper tried to help Charleston with his dilemma, "You know, Charlie, if you don't get your rest, you won't be able to run faster than your cousins." Now the threat of her cousins possibly beating her at anything struck a chord. Charlene took their everyday game of Hide and Seek seriously!

To sweeten the pot, Christopher added, "And maybe Aunt Savannah has some freshly baked bread. You know how you like to put butter on it and some of Grandma Georgie's strawberry preserves?"

"Absolutely!" Charlene shouted, vigorously nodding her head in agreement.

"Wait - so you can say a four-syllable word like absolutely, but can't say daddy?"

Sighing deeply, "Why is it so hard for you to say it right? Your name is Dada." Clearly frustrated at his lack of effort, Charlene sucked her teeth. Charleston was trying his best not to laugh at his daughter, but she was making it hard. The other men had no qualms about his daughter's wrath and laughed openly.

Something must have caught her attention because Charlene stretched her neck slightly, looking around her Uncle Christopher and waved towards the woods with the biggest smile. Her frustration now clearly forgotten.

Confused, Christopher asked, "Who are you waving at?"
"Luke," she stated matter of factly pointing to the woods behind them.

Charleston looked into the direction where Charlene waved and was greeted with a pair of eyes that were far too high up to belong to a dog. Actually, he was sure they belonged to a human. "Is anybody else seeing what I'm seeing? Crickets. His question was met with the sound of crickets from the men as they looked anywhere but the woods and “Charlene’s laughter."

CHAPTER 20

The Reckoning

Kedar knew something was off with his cousin when he left the room. Looking over at his uncle Zebulon, cocking an eyebrow emoting what he could not vocalize. The small board of predominantly family members that ran Black Caesar International sat in their Charlotte office board room, going over the previous quarter stats and looking at new contracts submitted for business.

The entire family was present, even Kedar's grandfather, which was highly unusual because he never left the islands unless he was heading for Florida. The unfortunate missteps of a son and favored grandson forced him to travel much further north than he would have liked. Even his father Edom was present, which in itself was a miracle and awkward at the same time.

Presenting was Astrid, his grandmother's smartly dressed assistant. Sleeveless blood red shirt and a colorful African print A-line skirt that reached her ankles completed her ensemble. Astrid was statuesque at good 6'1 without heels, slightly tanned skin, and long platinum blond hair. Anytime Kedar was in her presence, Astrid's hair was always in a bun with an ornate pin that held it in place. She was still polite, and from what he could tell, extremely smart. It was just weird seeing a person who was clearly not of African descent wearing African clothing. It just seemed... odd.

Hearing the door close again to the conference room brought Kedar's mind back to the presentation. Fernando walked across the room with a look of deadly intent on his face. Whatever was said while Fernando was in the hallway on that call must not have been good news.

There was no preamble or warning; he just started beating Victor's ass. For a moment, everyone sat there in shock, watching Fernando rain blow after blow – all to Victors face.

The first slap was so loud that it woke Zalmon Sr from the power nap he was taking while Astrid was presenting, and he nearly fell out of his chair, which sent Kedar into peals of laughter, but earned him a sharp look from his grandmother Rhoda. Finally waking up from his stupor, because Kedar was sure that was more than likely rum and not sweet tea he was sipping on earlier, he charged his oldest son, "Get that boy off my grandson!"

For the first time in a very long time, Kedar was speechless. He had no problems with Fernando moping the floor with Vic's face because he deserved it. He earned that right when he decided it was okay to basically enslave children for sex. His dumb ass should be in jail right now for what he did to those kids, but Kedar didn't get to make those decisions, plus he was weak like his father. He wouldn't have survived unless he traded family secrets for protection, and that could never happen.

“Uncle Zalmon Jr must have been out of his mind when he stood up if he thought that he was going to be able to tame the rage coming off Fernando," Kedar thought. Looking over at his Uncle Zebulon for next steps was a bust because he just sat there with a smirk on his face, then winked at Kedar. This was about to get truly ugly!

Feeling someone approaching from his back, Fernando pivoted quickly and advised with savage sincerity, “Touch me, and I will beat your mutherfucking ass like I'm about to finish beating your punk bitch of a son."

Hands up and backing away, Zalmon Jr questioned, "I think you've made your point - now you want to tell us why making this point was necessary son?"

Pulling the nine-millimeter from its holster, he aimed it at the center of his biological father's head, “You don't have the right to call me son. All you were was a sperm donor and a sorry one at that!”
Zebulon, hearing enough, spoke, “Zebulon Fernando Leblanc? Did I not teach you that we never have conversations with prey, especially with weapons pointed? You are not weak like your punk ass half-brother or his piece of shit father that you need to threaten anyone with anything but your presence. You are a Zelinka by blood and in spirit! Now act like one and holster that weapon. Now!”

Listening to one of the few men he respected immediately, Fernando put the safety back on and placed the gun back in its holster. Most of the folks in the room had moved away from the fray were still standing. Vic was going to need medical attention, but that would have to wait until the response to the accused crimes were given.

Breathing deep to take his temper down, Fernando looked at his grandmother Rhoda, "Adelinda and Charlene were attacked on the way home from Charlene's swim class. Little Charlie is safe, but Adelinda is missing."

Rhoda, who rarely ever showed her displeasure, slammed her hands against the table and leaned forward, "You two," pointing at her son Zalmon and her grandson Victor, "Did you have anything to do with this?"

Zalmon turned to his mother, hands raised in submission, "I swear to you on everything that I love mother, I had nothing to do with this! Victor has been at his mother's surrounded by security. There is no way he even had the people or connections to do anything like this."

Rhoda looked at her second oldest son hard for a few heartbeats and knew that he was telling the truth. She turned and looked at her husband and saw what others couldn't see, a nervous tick. It was a give-a-way that he'd had since the day he put on the wedding ring.

Anytime he was nervous, he twisted the ban on his finger. She knew in her heart that he was behind this, but she would not play her hand.
Bringing her house back to order, she did what she did best, lead.

"Fernando? You and Kedar head over to Adelinda's house and offer whatever services Charleston or Savannah may need. Zebulon? I need you with me."

Turning to look at her Victor and Zalmon Jr, "You better pray to whatever god you serve that nothing and I do mean nothing leads back to either of you!"

Showing no compassion whatsoever to the grandson she barely tolerated, "Now go clean yourself up and stop bleeding all over my carpet. Meeting adjourned!"

Without another word, Kedar and Fernando left to add whatever support they could, but something in his gut told Kedar this was just the beginning of fun things to come.

CHAPTER 21

Awkward

By the time Fernando drove down the lane that led to the Andino property, the yard was full of cars. The officers were still at the crime scene when they passed by, but they appeared to be wrapping up. They were met at the door by Earlene.

Fernando blushed just a little because, well, though she didn't realize it she was like a second mother to him. There were times when his mother was so weak due to her anemia that she couldn't get out of bed. It was during those times that Earlene took care of them forced his mother to go to the doctor so that she could get the medication she needed to be strong again; even paying the bill.

When they narrowed down the root cause, Earlene and Hugo made sure that her prescription and all the fresh vegetables they needed were always in the available. It was something he never forgot and why he always tried to look out for single mothers whenever he had the opportunity.

"Fernando," Earlene said with a smile, arms wide open awaiting her hug. He held him tight and rocked him just a little. Standing back with her hands now in his face, she leaned in and kissed his cheek then proceed grab his ear and yank it."

"Ummm Owww!" he cried with surprise. Still holding his ear while scolding what she considered her third son, "Don't ever stay away from me this long again! Are we clear?"

"Yes ma'am, we're crystal clear." Fernando said with what he couldn't help was a smile. It was a wonderful feeling to love and feel loved in return.

With her hand now around his waist, she looked at Kedar, "And you secret lover!" Earlene sang the words just like the song by Atlantic Starr, "No social awkwardness at all. Asa is in there with Charleston so gather yourself!"

Fernando looked everywhere but at his cousin. He knew if he did, he would burst out laughing. His saving grace came in the form of Hugo who was never far from his wife. Attached to his legs in an attempt to bring him down were to boys who looked to be around the age of six or seven based on their height.

"Mi Hijo," he whispered and hugged him tight. "Welcome!"

"Are those Christopher's boys?" Fernando asked looking at handsome young men.

"I guess me carrying them for nine months had nothing to do with it?" Savanah said laughingly. Opening the door, she ushered everyone in the house. Charleston, Idris and Del's brother Zaire are all in the family room where we have set up laptops and phones."

Looking at his shoulder, she noticed that Fernando had a backpack she was sure contained a laptop as well. Kedar had the same. Smiling at Kedar with imp like glee, "You must be Kedar. So glad to finally meet you."

Rubbing her hands together she looked at Earlene and laughed,

"Oh, this is too good!"

"Oh Asa? We have company!" Savannah chuckled.
Much to Savannah's disappointment, Asa didn't come to the door. Instead her older cousin came to the door with a message from her mother, "Hey guys! Come on in! Savannah? Your mother said if you don't come in the house right now and stop being petty, she was going to give you something to cackle about."

Now all this was said with a straight face, and the boys knew that

Grandma Georgie did not play… at all. Almost sing song like they chorused, “Uhoooooooh!”

That was back up my voice calling from inside the house, “Savannah Denise!” Savannah looked panicked which caused all adults that were outside to tip over with laughter and Savannah to respond with a low key, “Shit!”

The “shit” was not said low enough because the boys picked it up and ran with it. They detached themselves from their grandfather’s legs and ran back into the house to snitch. “Grandma Georgie! Grandma Georgie! Mommy said Shit!”

Savannah took off running after her sons, but everyone in the family knew that the only person that had a chance of catching them was Charlene. Screen door slamming and a “Hush your mouth!” could barely be heard over their laughter.

They needed that and Fernando “thanked the Maker” for it. It was one second in time in the last hour since he got the call that he was not about to lose his mind with worry.

Opening the door Elaine smiled, “Let me take you guys back. Charleston is waiting on you.”

The house smelled of baked bread, roasting vegetables along with something sweet. As Elaine guided them to the family room, both Kedar and Fernando noticed a beautiful older lady with honey blond hair sitting off to herself. In her lap were what looked to be quilting squares. Hearing their approach, she looked up and smiled, stopping both Fernando and Kedar in their tracks. Placing her items in the basket beside her, she stood and walked towards them. For Kedar it was the second time today he’d been dumbstruck.

“You must be Fernando?” She said with a radiant smile that reached her shining eyes. Feeling like a schoolboy Fernando mumbled, “Yes, ma’am. And this is my cousin Kedar.”

Turning her attention to Kedar she did the impossible, smiled even

brighter. Palms sweating, Kedar rubbed them against his slacks and stepped forward, holding out his hand. Instead his was greeted with open arms, "We're huggers! Get used to it!"
Fernando smiled; glad he was not the only one feeling uncomfortable with the affection shown. Turing his head, he saw the door that Elaine entered and decided to leave Kedar to his own devices.

Hugging Kedar tight Honey spoke to him, "You who have so much love to give, but never takes any for himself. I nor her father can never thank you enough for your kindness of shielding Asa. Don't worry though, your One is out there and the two of you together will be a force to reckon with!"

Stunned and not sure what to say, Kedar just nodded, slowly removing himself from her embrace. "Just keep straight and you'll walk right into the room."

Nodding again because he wasn't exactly sure what to say or do, Kedar walked in the direction he was given. Right before he reached the door, the one person he was anxious to see popped right into his vision as she was exiting the room. She was just as beautiful as she was when he last saw her.

"Hey Secret Lover!" she said with a wink.

"Shush your mouth young lady and you better not hug him," Charleston shouted from the room.

"Ummm – grown woman," Asa shouted back amongst the chuckles coming from the room. Doing the exact opposite of what her fiancé told her not to do, Asa wrapped her arms around him tight. Kedar, slightly panicked moved back a step, trying his best to make sure that in no way shape, form, or fashion their pelvises met.

"You really are trying to get my ass kicked," Kedar mumbled as he broke from the embrace.

"Not at all," Asa honestly replied. "You just looked like you needed it." With another wink and a smile Asa made her way towards the front of the house. Kedar watched her walk away and mentally kicked himself again for not stepping up when he had the chance. She gave the best hugs! A slight tug on his backpack strap startled him out of his revelry.

"Yes, she does give the best hugs!"
Those words were spoken from little Charlene but the question that Kedar was trying to figure out was if he had said them out loud.

"No, you didn't, but I heard them," Charlene said pointing to her head. "Please don't look at my mother that way. Yes, you had a chance and blew it, but I'm glad because then I wouldn't have Asa cause she's the best."

Apparently the third time was the charm because again – dumbstruck. How did this little girl know what I was thinking or what I felt for that matter? At a loss for words he asked the first logical thing that came to his mind, "How old are you?"

"Four," Charlene answered with a serious look on her face.
From somewhere in the house her Grandmother Georgie responded, "Charlene you are not four."

Stumping off and gearing up for an argument, "But Nana I'm gonna be four, why can't I just say that I'm four? David and Daniel are four! I wanna be four!"

Mouth open gawking, those behemoth twin boys were four, not six. In his mind he thought they were six. From prophesying women who for sure he thought was a past Ebony Beauty of the Week, to miniature giants, to little girls who could read expressions and thoughts. This day was just getting more complex as the seconds passed. There was just something not quite right about this family. Maybe he dodged a bullet? That thought made him feel marginally better until he walked into the room.

CHAPTER 22

Wake Up

Fernando had to admit that when he stepped into what was called the "Family Room," he was impressed. Hung on the walls were four fifty-inch televisions, three on a different channel one connected to a desktop. This set up had Del written all over it. Clapping his hand on his back, Charleston said, "Good to see you, man! And before you even ask, no one called. She left her phone in the car, so the police have it now."

Fernando looked around the room, taking in the area. "Impressive, right." It was Del's gift to Savannah and Christopher after Charlene returned to us."

A small smile flitted across his face, "This has Del written all over it," Fernando thought.

Charleston continued, "Since she bounces from house to house, we all thought it wise to set up office space so that she would be comfortable."

"You mean she talked so much shit about your lack of updated computer equipment that she shamed you into going out and buying new gear?" Fernando asked with a straight face.

Before Charleston could respond, Kedar walked in and parked at an empty spot at the table. He looked a little shaken up, so unlike his usual flappable self.

Forgetting he had his backpack on his shoulders, he stood and shrugged out of it, unzipping the bag and pulling out his laptop. Taking a cue from his cousin, Fernando slipped his backpack off his shoulder and took a seat. He was pretty sure that Del had them set up on a secure network, but you could never be too careful.

Looking up at Charleston, who was making his way around the table, "The only reason I'm not flipping tables is that I know my girl can handle her own."

Removing his laptop, Fernando popped it open and continued, "Why are there no police present? I thought that you said she was kidnapped?"

"The assumption from the police is that she is missing. They are not going to take the word of a little girl, and while they could see the footprints in the field, the bastards were smart enough to pick up the shell casing from the bullet," Charleston said frustrated.

Nodding and consuming the information, "That works in our favor. Now we can do what we do with no questions asked," Kedar chimed in, laptop now entirely up and running.

"True," Charleston agreed, looking up as Idris, Zaire, and Ezra entered the room.

Fernando and Kedar stood, acknowledging the elder in the room, Ezra, and waited for introductions.

Christopher who had stopped by the kitchen to get some bottled waters placed them on the table, "Fernando? You remember my grandfather Ezra? I'm not sure if you got to see him at mom's party."

Holding out his hand Ezra grabbed it the old way, the way of warriors, at the elbow. Fernando, not knowing what to do, mimicked his actions in kind, "It's a pleasure to see you again, sir."

Ezra looked at him for a moment and spoke slowly, "I see why she chose you. You let her be who she truly is and never tried to change her."

At a loss for what to say, Fernando remained silent, still grasping Ezra's arm.

Christopher interrupted the moment by continuing the introductions, "This Idris and Zaire. They work with a security firm that was recommended by Mak, Honey's brother.

Kedar held out his hand, shaking each of theirs, "Well, gentlemen, let's get to work. Do we have any new leads?"

“Possibly” Charleston said, looking at Christopher. Since the trespassing and attack on the property a while back, we decided to add cameras to the property. One of the cameras was pointed at the street and captured part of the incident. Idris was able to get the tag numbers and Earlene had them run for us."

“Anybody we know?”

“No,” the tags came back clean, but there is something else.

They each nodded and began to move back towards the table, each finding their seat. "Del and I had been toying with the idea of creating a bracelet that would be tough enough to withstand a child and not break yet slim sufficient to house a durable tracking device. We intended to give them to the kids as gifts, but we were still trying to beta test them. Del has one in her possession. Asa gave it to her today before she left to go to the museum.

"Is it active?" Idris asked, settling into his chair.
We are not sure, but it has a short battery life. She's been gone for roughly two hours now, and we don't know in what condition she left." Sliding over a laptop, "This is hers." Charleston tapped.

"While we dabble in technology, you and your family breathe it. The programming for the device is on her laptop, and quite frankly, none of us understand it.

Fernando slid the slim MacBook over to his side of the table and began to poke through the program. Dam, she was smart, Fernando thought.
It took him a few minutes to orient himself to her style of coding, but once he had the rhythm, verifying the device was not difficult.

"I'm in," he said distractedly. "It's currently registering as asleep, but if the device is near any phone that has wi-fi, I can send a single to activate it."

“We need to be ready for extraction,” Kedar said, taking a second look at the tag numbers Earlene couldn't trace.

Zaire spoke up for the first time, responding, "That will not be an issue. My team is on standby."

Fernando stopped mid keystroke and looked up at the man that claimed to be Del's brother. While he didn't necessarily see a family resemblance, he did see the same resolve in his eyes that Adelinda had. Nodding his head, Fernando went back to studying Del's work. There were so many questions he wanted to ask, but now was not the time.

"As soon as we have the coordinates, we take flight," Idris added.

"That son of a bitch," Kedar shouted, turning his laptop towards his cousin, he showed him what he had found.

Fernando's eyes glowed with rage, "Call the White Rose and let her know that it's about to be some sad signing." Turning towards Charleston, the de facto leader of this rescue mission, Fernando said, "On your mark."

Charleston looked at Idris and Zaire to confirm their readiness. Both gave their definitive response, yes.
"Wake her up," Charleston said with a smile.

EPILOGUE

The constant buzzing against her leg is what woke her up. Del's head was throbbing like someone had just dropped a compilation of DJ Magic Mike's best base hits. The pain was so intense that a tear slid unchecked down her face and she felt the bile building in her gut. Concussion, she may have a slight concussion, but she had to stay awake.

She had no clue where she was, but what she did know - someone was going to die. Del never opened her eyes and kept her body in a slumped position.

Moranda Jane Book Catalog

THE GIFT YOU GAVE

MORANDA JANE

VERACITY PUBLISHING PRESENTS

What Happens in NEW YORK

E.S. MCMILLAN

MORANDA JANE

GREEN LIGHT

MORANDA JANE

VERACITY PUBLISHING PRESENTS

BITTERSWEET

MORANDA JANE

Author Books Available on Amazon

What Happens in New York

Green Light

Bittersweet

www.ingramcontent.com/pod-product-compliance
Lightning Source LLC
LaVergne TN
LVHW091049150826
845673LV00002B/518